Match Wits with The Hardy Boys®!

Collect the Original
Hardy Boys Mystery Stories®
by Franklin W. Dixon

Celebrate 60 Years with the World's Greatest Super Sleuths!

THE HOODED HAWK MYSTERY

A trained peregrine falcon that the young detectives receive as a gift involves them in an exciting mystery. Imagine their astonishment when the swift-flying falcon brings down a homing pigeon carrying two precious rubies! Startling events that ensue indicate the gems are part of a ransom that has been paid for the release of a kidnapped student from India, who had come to the United States to complete his education. But Tava Nayyar, the son of a wealthy industrialist, is still being held captive.

Hoping to find a clue to Tava's whereabouts, the Hardys try to track down the owner of the ruby-bearing pigeon. Their every move, however, is thwarted by the dangerous criminals not only involved in the kidnapping, but also in the large-scale smuggling of aliens from India into the United States. How Frank and Joe eventually outwit their adversaries climaxes this thrill-packed mystery adventure.

Joe was snatched violently in mid-air

The Hardy Boys Mystery Stories®

THE
HOODED HAWK
MYSTERY

BY

FRANKLIN W. DIXON

GROSSET & DUNLAP
Publishers • New York
A member of The Putnam & Grosset Group

Printed on Recycled Paper

*The author hereby acknowledges
his gratitude to Dr. John J. Craighead, falconer
and wildlife research scientist
for his assistance in the preparation
of the falconry material
used in this story*

CONTENTS

CHAPTER I

Sender Unknown

"FRANK, come here!" Joe Hardy called excitedly to his brother from the front porch of their home.

It was early afternoon on a hot August day, but tall, eighteen-year-old Frank ran down the stairs at top speed. He knew from the tone of Joe's voice that something unusual was happening.

When he reached the porch, Frank stopped short and stared in amazement. An expressman, who stood there, grinning, had just delivered a burlap-covered crate and a package. Joe, blond and a year younger than Frank, had already removed the burlap. In the crate was a fine, proud-looking hawk.

"What a beauty!" Frank remarked. "Is it for us?"

"It says 'Frank and Joe Hardy, Elm Street, Bayport,'" the expressman answered, holding out a receipt for the boy's signature. As Frank wrote his

1

name, the man added, "This is a peregrine falcon and you'd better take good care of the young lady. She's valued at five hundred dollars."

"Wow!" Joe exclaimed. "That's an expensive bird!"

"Who sent her?" Frank asked. He looked at the package and read the name and address aloud, " 'Rahmud Ghapur, Washington, D.C.' Never heard of the man."

"Nor I," said Joe. "We'll ask Dad when he gets home."

As the expressman left, Frank opened the package. It contained several items which the boys knew were falconry equipment.

"Looks as though Mr. Ghapur expects us to become falconers," Frank declared. "But why?"

They searched for a note in the wrappings but found none. "We'll probably get a call or a letter of explanation," said Joe.

Frank agreed. "In the meantime, let's learn something about falcons. Dad has some books on the subject in his study."

All this time the blackish-blue hawk, with a black-barred creamy breast, had been sitting quietly in the crate, eying her new masters. Now she raised up, fluttered her wings, and cried *keer, keer,* as if she wanted to be released.

The boys carried the bird and her trappings through the hall and upstairs to Mr. Hardy's study. Here the famous detective had several file cabinets of criminal cases and photographs of underworld characters. Frank and Joe, endowed with natural sleuthing ability, had had many opportunities to work with their father. Frank was serious and an honor student at Bayport High, while Joe was rather impulsive but always dependable. Though they had different temperaments, the boys made an excellent team.

Joe found two volumes on falconry in his father's bookcase.

He handed one to Frank and began to flip through the pages of the other book. When he came to a series of pictures of the articles that the expressman had delivered, he said:

"Look, Frank, this is the leather hood. It's put over the hawk's head, so she'll sit quietly when she's being carried. And one of these bells is fastened to each of her legs so the owner can keep track of her movements."

Frank nodded and looked at an illustration in his book. "Here are those two leather straps. They're called *jesses*. One end of each jess is looped and tied around each of the hawk's legs. The free ends of the straps are fastened to a swivel, which consists of two rings connected by a bolt that allows each ring to turn separately. Both straps are tied to one of the rings and this long leather leash to the other ring. Pretty clever, Joe, because in that way the leash never gets tangled or twisted with the jesses."

Joe's eyes darted toward the crate. "Think we should try these trappings on Miss Peregrine?"

Frank laughed. "Maybe. But first, let's find out some more about falcons."

Joe, reading on, remarked, "She prefers pigeons to all other foods. But she can be brought back from a flight with any kind of meat or even the lure, if she's well trained." He picked up the lure, a short stick on the end of which was a thick bunch of feathers.

Frank, meanwhile, was studying the falconer's glove which had come in the package. "Joe," he said, "this glove must belong to someone from India or the Far East."

"How do you know?"

"My book said that in those countries falconers use right-handed gloves, while Europeans and Americans wear left-handed ones."

"Come to think of it," said Joe, "the name Rahmud Ghapur sounds Indian—or Far Eastern."

Frank agreed. "But the whole thing's still a mystery. Well, let's put the hawk's gear on."

As Frank held the equipment ready, Joe carefully opened the crate door. Although not sure how to handle the falcon, he quickly grabbed both legs so that the bird could not use her talons. She struggled while Frank fastened the jesses, then tied the straps and leash to the swivel. The boys kept a wary eye on the hawk, in case she should

*Joe held the falcon by both legs so she
could not lash out*

suddenly slash at them with her beak. But the bird made no such attempt.

"I guess the book was right when it said a falcon seldom uses its beak for defense," Joe remarked.

After Joe attached the little bells to the hawk's legs, Frank pulled on the glove, grasped both jesses, and lifted the falcon to his wrist. She sat there proud and defiant—a truly noble bird.

"So far, so good, Frank," Joe said. "Now what?"

"We'll take her outside and let her fly around a bit," his brother replied. "And let's get that old block perch Aunt Gertrude once used for her parrot. It's in the cellar."

"Good idea," replied Joe. "Miss Peregrine can rest on it when she's not flying. By the way, the book said that hawks should get plenty of exercise."

As they started downstairs, Joe suggested they show the bird to their Aunt Gertrude, who was in the kitchen.

The boys and their pet got only as far as the first-floor hall when suddenly the falcon yanked free and made a beeline for the living room. Just then the doorbell and the telephone rang. Frank sprang toward the door and Joe headed for the phone.

At that instant the kitchen door at the end of the hall opened and a tall, angular woman rushed forward. She was Mr. Hardy's sister, who lived with the family.

"Aunt Gertrude, watch the hawk in the living room, will you?" Joe requested, picking up the phone.

"Watch *what?*" his aunt exclaimed. But the bewildered woman received no further explanation. Joe was already speaking on the phone.

"Hello, Chet. Say, someone sent us a peregrine falcon."

"Great! What's that?" was the reply.

When Joe told him it was a hunting hawk, Chet said excitedly, "Bring it out to the farm, will you? I've never seen one."

"We will. Got to hang up because the bird's loose. See you later."

When Joe went into the living room, Aunt Gertrude was standing motionless staring at the hawk, which was now alternately rising and diving from windows to furniture.

"Joe!" Miss Hardy finally managed to exclaim. "Get that bird out of here at once!"

Frank stepped to the doorway of the living room and reported to Joe that the mail had come. There was a registered letter for Mr. Hardy, but nothing about the mysterious bird.

"What's going on here?" Aunt Gertrude demanded. "Where did you get that monstrous creature?"

"Well, we don't know the person who sent her—" Frank began. As he told Aunt Gertrude how the bird had arrived, the hawk suddenly lunged at her and grasped at her hands.

"Help! Take it away!" she cried frantically.

Joe yelled, "It's that piece of meat you're holding, Aunty! She thinks it's a lure!"

Aunt Gertrude looked at the raw meat she had absentmindedly brought from the kitchen. Frank took it from her hand and immediately the falcon returned to his glove to eat the meat.

Joe put his arm around Aunt Gertrude. "The falcon was only doing what she has been taught to do. Pieces of raw meat are used as lures for training these birds. The falcon didn't intend to harm you."

"Well, maybe you're right," Aunt Gertrude conceded grudgingly. "But falconers don't train their birds in a living room! Take her out of here."

With this ultimatum, Aunt Gertrude turned on her heel and stalked back to the kitchen.

Joe looked at Frank, grinned, and told him of Chet's invitation. "Let's take Miss Peregrine out to the farm," he said.

Chet Morton, a school chum, lived on a farm outside Bayport. A chubby, good-natured boy, he had frequently shared in the Hardys' adventures.

Frank took the hood from his pocket and attempted to put it over the head of the peregrine.

The bird flew off his gloved hand, but the jesses and leash held her. She soon stopped flapping and perched on the glove.

"Boy, this is harder than I thought," said Frank.

Joe, recalling what he had read in the falconry book on how to "break" a falcon to the hood, said, "We ought to lay a small piece of meat inside the hood before putting it on her."

Frank nodded. He said that the falcon is also fed a choice morsel of food after the hood is put on. Thus she connects a pleasant experience with hooding and does not struggle or fear the temporary blindness that the cover imposes.

After Joe had coaxed several scraps of raw meat from Aunt Gertrude, Frank managed to hood the hawk. He was awkward at it and resolved to practice until he could do it deftly.

As he carried the bird to the back yard, Joe ran to the cellar for the block perch. When he reappeared, Frank took the perch and said:

"I'll get the convertible and meet you in the driveway. You bring the hawk."

"Okay," Joe agreed, taking the glove and bird.

He paused to call good-by to Aunt Gertrude, then started toward the driveway.

A man, masked by a red-and-white bandanna and wearing a battered felt hat pulled low on his forehead, darted around a corner of the house and crashed into him!

The boy whirled and swung his free fist. But

the short, heavy-set stranger dodged and gave Joe a shove that sent him sprawling on the ground. At the same instant the man grabbed the leash, snatched the falcon, and sped down the driveway.

Quickly Joe got to his feet. Yelling to Frank to follow, he dashed off in pursuit of the thief!

CHAPTER II

Peregrine's Prize

By the time Joe had reached the foot of the Hardy driveway, the thief was half a block down Elm Street. The man forced the bird into a cloth sack as he ran. Then, seeing Joe in pursuit, he leaped a hedge and sprinted up a driveway between two houses.

As Joe reached it, a woman, leaning out a side window, gave a startled shriek. The masked man, evidently frightened, looked back to check Joe's progress. The side of his neck struck a clothesline, throwing him off balance, and Joe closed some of the gap between them.

"Drop that bird, you thief!" he shouted furiously.

The man staggered a few paces, then regained his balance. He jumped a low fence to the adjoining property and sped down its driveway, back to the street, still holding the bagged falcon!

Joe's shout and the woman's scream had attracted the attention of a policeman on Elm Street. As the thief reached the sidewalk, he slammed into the portly figure of Patrolman Smuff and dropped the sack.

"Grab him!" Joe yelled to the officer.

But the masked man, recovering himself quickly, side-stepped Smuff. Forgetting the bird, he cut across the street and disappeared into the dense, flower-covered foliage behind a house. Just then Frank swung the convertible alongside the curb. Joe picked up the sack and thrust it in beside his brother.

Patrolman Smuff had taken up the chase, and now Joe joined him. They searched the area thoroughly for two square blocks but were unable to find the fugitive or anyone who had seen him. As they retraced their steps to the convertible, Smuff asked:

"What's this all about, anyway?"

"That fellow tried to steal our bird."

"What kind of bird is it—a parrot?"

"No," Joe replied. "A peregrine falcon—a hawk."

"One of those hunting birds? I didn't know they had them around this part of the country."

"This one was sent to us. It's valuable."

The patrolman nodded. "Valuable, eh? Did you notice anything special about that thief?"

"Well," Joe replied, "his face was masked. But

this might help. When he grabbed the falcon, I got a good look at his hands. They were deeply tanned, so I guess he spends a lot of time outdoors. And he was wearing a carved ring with a ruby in it."

Patrolman Smuff jotted down this information. When they reached the convertible, he said goodby to the boys and hurried off.

As Joe climbed into the car, Frank gently lifted the falcon from the sack. Apparently, because the hood had prevented the bird from seeing, she had not become frightened by the experience.

"Since Miss Peregrine seems to feel okay," Frank said, "let's go on to Chet's as we planned."

With the falcon perched on Joe's wrist, the boys rode out of town. A short time later they arrived at the Morton farm. They saw Chet near a corner of the barn, making repairs on a door. The stout boy was alternately munching on an apple and hammering.

"Wow!" Joe grinned. "Chet's working!"

Although the Hardys needled their easygoing pal a great deal, they were close friends. Chet had been helping them ever since the days of their first mystery, *The Tower Treasure*. Just recently, in the boys' latest case, *The Yellow Feather Mystery*, his skill with machinery and the operation of his motor sled had been instrumental in rescuing the Hardys from death in a sealed-up ice fort.

As Chet hurried over to see his friends, he called

cheerfully, "Hi, fellows! Did you bring the hawk?"

The Hardys slid out of the car, and the falcon was transferred to Frank's wrist.

"Pretty neat!" Chet remarked. "Let's see her without her hat." He reached out to remove it.

"Wait a minute," said Frank. "She's been through a rugged experience this afternoon," and he told Chet what had happened.

Chet's eyebrows lifted. "Sounds like the beginning of another mystery for you fellows."

"Sure does," said Joe.

Chet looked at the hawk. "She seems really tame," he commented.

"She is," Joe replied as Frank removed the hood from the falcon.

Chet studied the notched beak and the long, tapered wings, which Frank said were characteristic of all falcons. "She's streamlined, all right," he declared.

"Yes, and she's a powerful flier," Joe added. "According to one of Dad's books, she's very courageous—but gentle, too. Notice her dark eyes and the way she holds her head up. The ancient falconers called the peregrines noble and gentle birds. This breed was the prize of medieval kings."

Chet was visibly impressed. "How about a trial flight?"

At that moment his sister Iola appeared on the

back porch of the farmhouse and called, "Hi, boys! Would you like some lemonade?"

Frank waved and said that he would have some later. But Joe immediately hurried toward the house. The slender, pretty girl, with dark hair and eyes, was his date on many occasions as well as a capable sleuthing assistant.

Meanwhile, as they walked toward an open field, Chet asked Frank to let him fly the falcon.

"Better let me try it first," said Frank. "I'm not sure how successful I'll be, since all I know about falconry is what I read in the book."

He stopped, unfastened each jess from the swivel, and then, with a somewhat awkward movement of the glove, he threw the hawk into the air. With long, powerful wing beats the falcon circled, rising higher and higher until she was merely a dot above them in the sky.

"Now what?" Chet asked.

"See this," said Frank, holding out the feathered lure.

"What on earth is that?"

"According to the book, the falconer waves this lure in the air and the falcon immediately drops earthward and strikes it."

"You mean she'll come back to that thing?" Chet asked incredulously.

Frank nodded, watching the hawk intently. "See how she keeps circling us!" he exclaimed.

"That's called 'waiting on.' She'll maintain her pitch there until I call her back, either by waving the lure or flushing a bird."

Frank swung the lure several times, then let it drop to the ground. Immediately the falcon turned and plummeted toward them at terrific speed.

"She's stooping!" yelled Frank. "Listen to the wind whistle through her feathers!"

The falcon came within a foot of striking the lure, then swung upward and mounted almost to her previous height in the sky.

"That was sensational!" breathed Chet.

The falcon made a wide circle and then headed off with deep, powerful wing beats.

"Hey! She's flying away!" Chet cried out.

"No," said Frank. "Look! She's after something!"

"It's a pigeon!" Chet gripped his friend's arm.

"I'll call the falcon to the lure," Frank said tersely.

But it was already too late. With unbelievable speed the falcon closed the distance and then streaked earthward, striking the pigeon in midair.

The boys saw a tuft of feathers fly and heard the sharp report of the impact. The pigeon dropped to the ground, and the falcon, after mounting from her stoop, dropped down again to claim her prize

Frank and Chet went toward the two birds, hoping to rescue the pigeon. Slowly, in order not to frighten the hawk, Frank reached for the jesses. With wings and tail spread, the bird looked defiantly at him but made no attempt to fly off. The boy secured the jesses and put on the leash.

"Too bad," said Frank, "but the pigeon's dead."

He stroked the hawk, and then slowly lifted both the pigeon and falcon. As he did, he saw a small red capsule on one of the pigeon's legs.

"Gosh, it's a carrier pigeon!" exclaimed Chet.

Frank, concerned that the falcon had killed someone's prized bird, asked Chet to twist the cap off the small container. Chet did so and shook it gingerly over the palm of his hand. To the boys' amazement, instead of a message, out fell two glittering red stones.

"That's strange," Frank remarked.

Joe, who had been watching the falcon's performance, joined his brother and Chet. The trio bent over the stones in Chet's hands. Frank asked Joe to check the pigeon's other leg for an identification band.

"Nothing here," he reported.

Frank rubbed his fingers over the stones and recognized an oily feel to them.

"I believe that these are rubies—valuable rubies!"

CHAPTER III

Smugglers

"Rubies!" Chet exclaimed in amazement. Then he laughed. "You're fooling, Frank. In fact, if those stones are anything but colored glass, I'll treat you both to a dinner."

Joe grinned. "We couldn't refuse an offer like that!"

"Let's get a jeweler's opinion!" Frank urged.

Wrapping the stones in a handkerchief, he put them into a pocket of his sports jacket. The boys buried the pigeon, then drove to the center of Bayport and parked close to Bickford's Jewelry Store. While Joe stayed with the falcon, Frank and Chet went into the shop. The owner, Arthur Bickford, knew them well. He looked up and smiled.

"Well, what brings you here?"

Frank opened the handkerchief and revealed

the two red stones. "We found these," he said, "and we'd like you to tell us whether or not they're genuine."

Bickford studied the gems for a moment, ran them through his fingers, then picked up his eyepiece. He peered at the stones one at a time, then marveled, "I've never seen more flawless rubies. They're quite valuable. Where'd you get them?"

Frank evaded the question but remarked, "If they're so valuable, we'd better turn them over to the police."

The two boys thanked the jeweler and returned to the convertible. As Frank and Joe were discussing their great find, Chet reminded them that the rubies had been found on his farm.

"That's right," Joe admitted, "so it means you'll have to help solve the mystery."

Chet winced at the thought of the work involved, but said, "Sure, and then I'll get my share of the reward for the rubies."

Frank chuckled. "And you can use the money to treat us to dinner."

"Okay, okay," Chet said with a grin. "Any time you say."

"Let's make it right after we turn these gems over to Chief Collig," Joe said. "Chet, will you stay here to mind the falcon?"

The Hardys crossed the street to police headquarters, and five minutes later were seated in Chief Ezra Collig's office.

"What mystery have you boys turned up now?" the officer asked with a smile.

Frank handed over the rubies. "Mr. Bickford told us these are valuable stones. Have you had a report of any robbery involving gems like these?"

Chief Collig said he could not recall any, but would ask one of his detectives, and buzzed for him.

"Nothing like that has been reported missing," the detective replied to Frank's inquiry. "And we'd sure hear about such a theft from other departments."

The chief thanked him and the man withdrew. They talked about the stones and the carrier pigeon for some time but could come to no conclusions.

The boys left the rubies with Chief Collig for safekeeping. When they rejoined Chet, they decided to forego his dinner treat for the time being and return home, since it was time to feed the hawk. Chet suggested that they let him off at his father's real-estate office. Mr. Morton would drive him back to the farm.

When Frank and Joe reached home their mother was setting the table for dinner. Mrs. Hardy was a small, slim woman with blond hair and sparkling blue eyes.

"What a noble-looking bird!" she remarked. "Your aunt told me all about her."

Aunt Gertrude appeared from the kitchen just as Frank noticed there was a plate at his father's place.

"Dad's home from Washington!" he cried out.

"He's in town all right," Aunt Gertrude replied, adding with a frown, "And when he hears about that vicious hawk you boys have, he's not going to like it."

"Perhaps he won't mind when we tell him about the rubies our bird got for us," Frank said, grinning.

When the boys related the story, the women gasped in amazement.

At Aunt Gertrude's insistence, Frank and Joe took the falcon to the garage. They set up the block perch and put the falcon on it. The boys fed her some parrot seed, set the burglar alarm, and locked the door.

Fenton Hardy arrived a few minutes later. He was a tall, dark, distinguished-looking man. His sons loved his keen sense of humor and admired his brilliant mind. Mr. Hardy's preoccupied manner as the family sat down to dinner could mean only one thing. He was busy on an important case.

Sensing his sons' curiosity, he said, "I've been asked to help on an interesting problem which has the authorities baffled. Immigration officials have learned of the large-scale smuggling of aliens from India into the United States somewhere along the Atlantic coast. One suspected spot is Bayport."

"Bayport!" Frank repeated in astonishment, adding, "Any other clues?"

"None. But maybe you boys can find some," Mr. Hardy replied with a twinkle in his eye. "I'm working on another case right now that I'll have to finish before I can concentrate on this smuggling racket."

"In other words, Dad, you're asking Joe and me to start from scratch. No leads or anything?"

"You know I wouldn't do that, son," Fenton Hardy replied, smiling. "I have two possible leads.

"While I was in Washington, I called on an old friend—an Indian importer. I talked with him about the illegal entry of aliens from his country and told him I was going to ask you boys to work on the case. He naturally frowns on anything that will detract from his country's good reputation, and has offered to assist in every way he can."

"Did he give you any leads?" Frank asked.

"No, but I mentioned to him that there must be some means of communication between the smugglers and their confederates on shore. We eliminated radio and telegraph because they could be monitored. But it occurred to me that secret messages, instructing the contact here to pick up the smuggled men, might be sent by carrier pigeons from the ships offshore to the racketeers' hideout on land. Ghapur agreed."

"Ghapur!" Joe burst out. "Dad, is your Indian friend's name Rahmud Ghapur?"

"Why, yes, son," Mr. Hardy answered.

The boys told their father about the falcon they had received from Ghapur, the attempted theft of the bird, and the ruby-bearing carrier pigeon which the peregrine had downed.

"That's very interesting," Mr. Hardy said. "I'll phone Ghapur at once."

Fortunately the importer was at home. The detective talked with him for some time, then returned to the table.

"Mr. Ghapur says he sent the falcon to aid you boys in bringing down pigeons you might be suspicious of. He mailed a letter of explanation. Didn't it arrive?"

"No," Frank replied, adding thoughtfully, "The letter could have been intercepted by the smugglers if they suspected what the falcon was to be used for."

"True," Mr. Hardy declared. "Ghapur asked you boys to get in touch with a fellow countryman of his who lives here in Bayport. He's Ahmed, the rug dealer. You know him. He'll teach you how to handle the falcon properly."

This statement caused Aunt Gertrude to speak up sharply, deploring the fact that the boys were getting involved in such a cruel sport.

"Aunty," said Frank, "it's in the line of duty. And anyway, wild hawks eat ten times as many pigeons and other birds in a year than we'd let a trained falcon like Miss Peregrine go after."

"Humph!" Aunt Gertrude was unconvinced, and was about to continue her tirade when Mrs. Hardy arose and started clearing the table. Her husband and sons got up too and went to the garage to see the falcon. After examining her trappings, Mr. Hardy said with a smile:

"It will be rather unique to solve a mystery with a hooded hawk."

"Yes," agreed Frank. "Dad, do you think there might be a tie-in between the smugglers of aliens and the rubies?"

"Yes, I do," Mr. Hardy replied. "And I have a hunch we'll find that carrier pigeons are the link between our two mysteries."

They talked for a while longer, then Fenton Hardy concluded with, "Well, boys, it will have to be your job for the time being to solve these mysteries. I must get back on my other case. From time to time I'll be in touch with you, though."

"You're leaving?" Joe asked.

"Yes. I'm flying back to Washington. Will you drive me to the airport?"

"Certainly, Dad."

After the boys had dropped Mr. Hardy at the airport, Joe suggested, "Let's phone Ahmed. It's not too late, and I'd like to get to work."

"Good idea," replied Frank. "We should know more about training and flying the bird. We were just lucky this afternoon."

He put through a call to the elderly rug merchant. After identifying himself, Frank told him about the message from Rahmud Ghapur.

Though surprised, Ahmed gladly consented to teach the Hardys how to handle the falcon. He said that they must first obtain permission from the State Fish and Game Department to fly the hawk. It was agreed that the boys would do this the next morning, then the three would drive out to the country.

"The Morton farm is a good place," Frank suggested.

At the Bayport office of the Fish and Game Department the next day, the clerk looked quizzical when the boys made their request. But when they explained it was in connection with one of their father's cases, he gave them each special hunting permits.

With their falcon and a bag containing its equipment, the Hardys drove to Ahmed's place of business. The rug dealer was standing in the doorway, waiting for them. He was close to sixty years old, but straight as a spear and lithe in his movements.

When the elderly man was seated in the car, he turned his attention to the hawk. Putting on the gauntlet, Ahmed wristed the bird. As he stroked it, he remarked:

"This hawk is well trained. As a fledgling she was probably lured into a net, then hooded, and carried constantly on the glove until she lost her fear of man and became tame. This is called 'manning.'

"The trainer strokes her, talks gently to her, and feeds her. The falcon becomes completely dependent on her master and learns that he intends no harm. Gradually she is made hungry or 'keen' and thus learns to respond to the falconer. At first she jumps a short distance to the glove for food. Gradually the distance is increased until she is flying several hundred yards on a string. Finally she can be flown free."

"Then she's actually trained through her appetite?" Frank asked.

"Yes," Ahmed replied. "And a young bird's instincts are channeled so that she performs in a natural way for her trainer. She is never taught to do anything that she would not normally do in the wild."

"Will she bring her quarry back to her master?" Joe queried.

"No," Ahmed replied. "She goes to the ground with her kill, then the falconer hurries to his bird. The hawk does not come to him. However, if the bird misses her quarry, she will return to the lure to be fed."

"It's a complicated sport," Frank remarked. "And I can see why it requires lots of time and patience."

"Well, one thing we do know," Joe spoke up. "Pigeons are a hawk's favorite food." He grinned.

"But we didn't have a squab in our refrigerator, so I gave her raw oatmeal and parrot seed for breakfast."

Ahmed smiled. "You'll have to feed her starlings, sparrows, mice, and lean beef. It's obvious that she is used to people and normal sounds, since neither of these bother her."

When they arrived at the Morton farm Iola informed them that Chet had gone to market with a load of sweet corn. She promised to tell him where the Hardys were as soon as he came in.

The visitors strolled to one of the large open fields and Ahmed began his instruction. He suggested that Frank undertake flying the hawk first. Compared to Ahmed's dexterity, the boy felt very clumsy in putting on and taking off the jesses and the hood. He also felt that due to his inexperience the hawk must be tiring from the procedure.

"Let's give the poor bird a rest," he suggested. "In the meantime, I'd like to learn more about the history of falconry."

Ahmed agreed, and holding the falcon, he walked around the field with the Hardys. As they strolled along, the rug dealer told them about the short-winged hawks that are flown from the fist at such quarry as game birds and rabbits.

"These birds," Ahmed said, "such as the goshawk, the sharp-shinned hawk, and the Cooper's hawk are the best ones for a beginner to practice with.

"In my country, and in yours too, the peregrine falcon is considered the prize bird and only experienced falconers capture and train them. It is an unwritten law that novice falconers start on the less noble birds, and as they gain experience, they earn the right to train the peregrines."

"We're fortunate to start off with a trained one," said Joe.

"Indeed you are," replied Ahmed.

As the three walked back across the field, Ahmed gave the boys additional pointers on the care of their falcon, advising them to keep the bird with them at all times, so that she would recognize them as her masters.

"Remember," he said, "to put water out for her bath, to keep her in the shade, and to place her perch where she can't get tangled up. Above all," he cautioned, "be kind and gentle to her and she will reciprocate. Always bear in mind that she puts great trust in you; don't fail her."

Frank and Joe were assuring him that they would certainly do their best when they heard a loud yell.

"Hey, fellows!" It was Chet, standing at the edge of the field and waving at them. "Quick! I've got news!"

"Good or bad?" Joe shouted back as he and Frank started running toward their friend.

"Don't know. But you'll find out at police headquarters!"

CHAPTER IV

A Suspicious Sailor

FRANK and Joe sprinted across the field to where Chet was waiting for them.

"What's this news from police headquarters about?" Joe demanded excitedly.

"All I know," said the stout boy, "is the department called and said you should report there pronto!"

The same thoughts flashed through the brothers' minds: Was it news of the rubies or of Joe's masked assailant?

"We're on our way," said Joe as Ahmed caught up to them, the falcon still on his wrist.

They hurried to the convertible and drove to Bayport. After leaving Ahmed at his shop, the boys headed for police headquarters. Frank remained in the car with the falcon while Joe went inside. Officer Smuff was waiting for him.

"You have news for us?" Joe asked.

Smuff nodded. "I saw a man lurking around your house. Swarthy complexion, red-and-white bandanna around his neck, and wearing a battered felt hat."

"You mean you've caught our hawk thief?"

"I don't know if he's the one, Joe. You'll have to identify him. But he certainly fitted your description!"

Smuff led the boy into a small room. A sun-tanned figure slouched on a bench. When the man saw Joe, he jumped up.

"Am I glad you're here," he said with a slight Italian accent. "I went to your house and looked for the lawn mower, and this cop took me down here for I don't know what!"

Joe grinned. "Sorry, Nicolo. It's a case of mistaken identity!"

Nicolo looked at the policeman defiantly. "See? I told you!"

"Nicolo is our gardener," Joe explained to Smuff. "He comes every week to cut the lawn."

Smuff shrugged and apologized to the man.

"That's okay," Nicolo said when he heard about the hawk thief. "Now can I go back to work?"

Since it was nearly lunchtime, the boys drove Nicolo to the Hardy home. As Joe carried the falcon toward the back door, Mrs. Hardy appeared and said:

"Please don't bring the hawk into the house. It will only upset your Aunt Gertrude."

Frank took the hawk to its perch in the garage, set the burglar alarm, and locked the door. He had just sat down at the table for lunch when Joe appeared, carrying a volume of the encyclopedia with him.

"It says here, 'Most hawks, peregrines especially, require a bath,'" Joe read. " 'The end of a cask, sawed off to give a depth of six inches, makes a good tub. Peregrines which are used to "waiting on" require a bath at least twice a week.'"

" 'Waiting on'! You certainly do have to wait on them!" Aunt Gertrude retorted.

Frank and Joe exchanged grins, then told their aunt what the term meant. Frank read on from the book in his brother's hands. " 'If the bath is neglected, the falcon is inclined to soar when flown, and may even break away in search of water, and so be lost.'"

Miss Hardy cleared her throat with a loud *harrumph*, which ended further conversation about the hawk.

After lunch the boys made a cask tub for the falcon and let her bathe. Then they laid plans for beginning their work on the case Mr. Hardy had outlined for them.

"My guess is," said Frank, "that anyone smuggling immigrants into the country would probably do it after dark. Let's take the *Sleuth* out in the bay this evening and scout around for a few hours."

"Good idea," Joe agreed. "But remember, Miss Peregrine has to go along."

About seven-thirty the boys changed to old pants and sweaters, then hurried to the garage. Joe put on the gauntlet and signaled for the hawk to come to his wrist. When the bird was in place, he hooded it, and Frank drove to their boathouse.

After climbing aboard the sleek motorboat, Joe attached the bird's leash to the jesses on her legs and set her on a short horizontal pole in the wheel cabin, which was intended for raincoats and jackets. The bird accepted the roost readily.

Moments later Frank had the *Sleuth* under way. As the craft knifed smoothly through the water, the boys were pleased to see that the falcon remained quiet. Presently Joe asked:

"What kind of boat do you think we ought to look for out here?"

"I surmise that the smugglers would come close to the twelve-mile limit in a large boat," his brother replied. "Then they contact the shore and make arrangements to have the immigrants transported the rest of the way in a speedboat."

"Sounds logical," Joe agreed.

Feeling a drop of rain, Joe looked up at the sky. In the distance he spotted a pigeon flying toward land. Grabbing binoculars, he trained them on the bird. Frank, too, had seen the pigeon. Both boys wondered if it were a carrier.

"Suppose we let the hawk bring it down on the beach," Joe suggested.

"It might help us more to know where the bird is going, so we can locate the owner," Frank asserted. "Get the pigeon's direction, Joe."

He handed his brother a pocket compass. Joe balanced it on his hand, and compensating for the bobbing of the speedboat, studied the movements of the settling needle carefully.

Frank and Joe were well aware that carrier pigeons' actions are fairly predictable. When turned loose at their departure point, they fly straight up into the air, circle, pick up the beam to their home cote, and set off in a straight line.

By the speed and assurance with which the pigeon overhead was flying, the boys were convinced that it was making a beeline for home. When the bird was finally out of sight, Joe remarked:

"The pigeon was heading straight southwest. The question is, How far inland is it going?"

"We have a starting point for our search, anyway," Frank commented. "Hey, that pigeon at Chet's farm was headed in a southwest direction, too."

"Right. And now, with a possible clue to the smugglers' mainland hideout, let's do a bit of aerial sleuthing."

"First thing tomorrow."

Presently Frank turned the wheel over to Joe. He was just about to head into the ocean when Joe said:

"We have company."

A deep-sea fishing cruiser was coming toward them from the open sea. Frank picked up the glasses and read the name *Daisy K*. The Hardys recognized this as a weather-beaten sports fishing craft used for charter trips. It was frequently tied up in Bayport. But they knew nothing about its owner.

"Think she's suspicious?" Joe asked.

"Take a look at the sailor leaning over the rail on the starboard side," Frank urged excitedly.

As the *Daisy K* approached, Joe adjusted the glasses and peered at the heavy-set, dark-skinned man, who had piercing black eyes. Both of the man's hands were resting on the rail, and at first glance he appeared to be just a tired sailor relaxing after a long, wearing day's work.

"What do you think, Joe?"

"Same as you do."

For a reason they could not explain, the boys felt sure that this was the mysterious masked man who had tried to steal the falcon! But on neither of his hands was the telltale ruby ring. In a moment the *Daisy K* had passed the *Sleuth*.

"I don't suppose," said Joe, "that we ought to suspect every sun-tanned stranger. I have a funny feeling, though, that he is our man. Shall we follow him?"

"We haven't a shred of evidence against the fellow, Joe—and anyway, we know where to find him if we want him. I'd rather keep looking out here for clues to the smugglers."

"Okay."

It was choppy on the open sea, and as darkness settled, the wind grew strong.

"I guess we'd better go back," Frank proposed. "The waves are getting pretty high and I don't think Miss Peregrine likes it!"

The hawk was finding it hard to retain her perch and finally Frank took the bird on his wrist. "Too bad we couldn't continue our sleuthing," he remarked. "But then, it would be impossible for us to get near another boat on a night like this."

About half an hour later the Hardys nosed the *Sleuth* into the slip of their boathouse. Frank set the falcon back on her pole perch, and had just closed the door behind them when there was a low rumble in one corner of the boathouse. The next instant there came a blinding flash, followed by a sharp explosion that rocked the building!

A sheet of flame roared up the walls and across the boathouse directly toward the *Sleuth!*

CHAPTER V

Indian Intrigue

STUNNED, the Hardys could see no escape from the flash fire which had trapped them in their boathouse. As the initial shock wore off, Frank cried:

"Open the door, Joe!"

The youth swung it up as Frank gunned the boat's motor. The *Sleuth* shot backward into open water a split second before the fire reached its prow.

"Whew!" said Joe. "Sabotage!"

His brother nodded as he docked nearby. Joe quickly fastened the hawk's leash to a rowboat painter while Frank grabbed a fire extinguisher from the *Sleuth*. Both boys raced back to their boathouse.

Behind them, the boys could hear a watchman shout, "What's wrong over there?"

"Fire!" Frank yelled. "Give us a hand!"

One glance around the boathouse told the Hardys that a single fire extinguisher would do little good. Nevertheless, Frank played it around until it was empty.

Joe ran outside and called the fire department from a public phone. Then he looked for some clue to the fire's origin. Near the side door he noticed a small wad of newspaper on the floor. He put it into his pocket.

At that moment the watchman ran up with a hand line from a nearby hydrant, and the blaze was soon extinguished. But the boathouse was badly damaged.

The Bayport fire engines turned into the waterfront street. When the chief discovered that things were under control, he sent his men back but remained himself to talk to the boys.

"How did the fire start?" he asked.

"There was an explosion," Joe replied and told what had happened. After a quick inspection, the chief agreed that an arsonist was responsible.

When the fire chief had left and the watchman had returned to his shack, Joe pulled the wad of paper from his pocket. "This might tell us something," he said to Frank. "But it's too dark to read here."

The boys went to their boat and got a flashlight. To their amazement they saw that the printing was in a strange, oriental-looking script.

"It might have been printed in India," Frank

said, "and if so, one of the smugglers could have set the fire."

"There's one man who can tell us if you're right," Joe reflected. "Ahmed."

"Think he'll be up this late?"

They decided that it would be worth a try. As they were about to leave, Joe suddenly halted and exclaimed, "Wait! We almost forgot the hawk!"

While he went to retrieve the falcon, Frank made arrangements with the watchman to leave the *Sleuth* at another dock. Then they drove to the small bungalow where Ahmed lived. The house was brightly lighted. They rang the bell, and the rug dealer admitted the boys and their falcon. He led them into an attractive living room, furnished in oriental style.

Frank and Joe took turns supplying Ahmed with the details of their exploits. Frowning in concern, he spread the sheet of newspaper on a bronze table. He scanned the lines closely, then turned to his callers.

"It is part of a story which reports that Tava, the son of Satish Nayyar, a well-known industrialist from the Province of Hatavab where I come from, will visit the United States. The boy is eighteen and is to finish his education in this country. Satish Nayyar is one of the richest men in India and has a reputation of being a great humanitarian as well. Incidentally, the dateline on this paper is Delhi, two months past."

Ahmed glanced over the rest of the newspaper but found nothing in any of the other items that could be interpreted as a clue to the identity of the arsonist.

Frank asked, "How many persons around Bayport would be likely to read a newspaper from India?"

"A dozen, perhaps. I have six men from Delhi working for me, and there must be an equal number employed on the fishing boats in the vicinity."

"Thank you very much, Ahmed," Frank said, rising. "This information may shed some light on our case."

The Hardys said good night, returned to their car, and headed for home.

They were up early the next morning. After breakfast Frank telephoned a builder, who agreed to start repairing the boathouse shortly. Then Frank called the local airport and found that they would have to postpone their aerial search for the smugglers' hideout, since the helicopter pilot was busy for the rest of that day.

Later that morning, Frank and Joe had a conference with Chief Collig about the fire and left the sheet from the Delhi newspaper with him. The chief promised to look into the matter.

"Joe," Frank said as they left police headquarters, "if we're going to use our hawk to help solve the mystery, we'd better do some more practicing."

"Right. Let's go out to Chet's after lunch."

The Hardys decided to walk and carry the bird, since this would give the falcon an opportunity to become accustomed to them. Frank hooded Miss Peregrine as Joe picked up the falconer's bag, and they started out.

The boys talked all the way, knowing that it was important for the falcon to become familiar with their voices and thus obey them more promptly. By now, she came readily to either boy's fist for food, as well as to the lure.

When they arrived at the Morton farm, Mrs. Morton told them that Chet had gone to town but was expected back soon. They left a message for Chet to join them, and immediately set off for the isolated spot where they would release the falcon. There, Joe unhooded the bird and removed the leash. He then directed her attention to several crows which were flying over a clump of trees and threw her off.

Instinct seemed to warn the crows, however, for almost as soon as the falcon had left Joe's glove, they flew into a thicket. The hawk circled for a while, then climbed upward into the sky until she appeared no larger than a swallow.

"Maybe we're going to lose her," Joe said, worried.

"I don't believe so," Frank reassured him. "She's 'waiting on,' expecting us to flush more suitable quarry for her to strike."

"Well, we'll give her some," said Joe, taking the lure from the falconer's bag and waving it.

"She's coming back!" Frank cried.

Both boys watched a tiny speck hurtling toward them, growing larger by the second. In a long, graceful swoop the falcon came in and struck the lure with a smack. Joe held it firmly and the hawk came to rest. He offered her some raw meat, then hooded her and set the bird on his wrist.

Just then Frank spotted Iola Morton running toward them. When she reached the Hardys, she paused for breath, then blurted out:

"Your father's home! He's been trying to reach you. Something important has come up about your new case!"

Surprised to learn that their father was back so soon from Washington, the boys dashed to the Morton house and called home.

"What's up, Dad?" Frank asked excitedly.

"I've just received a phone call from Mr. Gha-pur. He's coming here from Washington with a friend from India who has a strange story to tell us."

"What is it?"

"The matter was too confidential to discuss over the telephone, Frank. The men will arrive tonight. I thought you boys would want to be on hand."

"We'll be there," Frank promised.

As Frank put down the phone, Chet appeared

with a huge container of ice cream. Frank told Chet of the meeting to be held at the Hardy home that evening.

"Maybe it's about our rubies," their stout friend suggested.

As dinnertime approached, Chet drove the Hardys and their falcon home in his jalopy.

"Let me know what happens, fellows," he called, waving good-by.

Fenton Hardy was waiting. "Our callers will arrive about nine o'clock," he said.

Night had closed in and they were waiting for the front doorbell to ring, when a knock sounded on the back door. The boys and their father hurried to the kitchen and Fenton Hardy opened the door. Two men were standing there.

"Mr. Ghapur!" the detective exclaimed.

"We thought we were being followed," the importer explained, stepping in. "Please pardon this strange way of entering your home."

Rahmud Ghapur was a dark-complexioned man, about fifty years old, with lines at his temples that indicated a normally jovial disposition. Right now, however, his expression was tempered by the seriousness of the situation. His companion, about ten years younger, was introduced as Mr. Delhi, a trusted emissary and cousin of Satish Nayyar.

Ghapur added that the Indian, who retained a

high government post, had assumed the name Delhi because he wished to remain incognito while in the United States.

"My real name is Bhagnav," Mr. Delhi said.

Mr. Hardy shook hands with him and introduced his sons. "We'll go up to my study," he said, "where we can be sure that our discussion will not be overheard by possible eavesdroppers at our doors or windows."

He led the way to the second floor. After everyone was seated, Frank offered to bring the falcon to Mr. Ghapur, but the man advised against it.

"If the bird were to see me," he said, "the fine progress you have made with her might be undone."

Ghapur turned to his companion. "Please tell your story," he requested.

Mr. Delhi began with a question. "Had you heard that Tava Nayyar was on his way to the United States in order to complete his education?"

"We learned it last night from a newspaper clipping," Frank replied, and told of their adventure in the boathouse.

"He arrived in New York all right," Mr. Delhi went on. "Then he was kidnapped!"

"Kidnapped!" chorused the Hardys, and Joe added, "When?"

"About a month ago. Ransom was demanded in rubies. We received orders to leave the gems in a certain place in India. The orders were carried out and the rubies picked up. But Tava has not been released."

"You haven't heard anything?" Frank asked.

"Oh, yes. We have received a new ransom note which demands that more rubies be left at the designated spot. The note, like the first one, threatens Tava with death if payment is not made or if the story of his kidnapping is published."

Mr. Delhi paused. "I—I am afraid Tava may not even now be alive," he said somberly. "But his father has not given up hope."

Rahmud Ghapur picked up the story. "Satish Nayyar sent Mr. Delhi to this country to see if he could track down the kidnappers. Since I am a native of the same province, he came to me for help. I suggested that we get in touch with you. Can you and your sons look into this matter for us?"

"We'll be glad to," Fenton Hardy assured them. "In fact, my boys may have picked up a clue already."

"Yes? How so?" both visitors asked in amazement.

Frank and Joe told them of the precious rubies from the carrier pigeon brought down by the hawk.

The Indians were astounded to hear this news and agreed that the rubies might very well be part of the ransom. They thought, too, that the missing youth might be held at the place from which the pigeon had been released or where it was heading.

"More likely it's the latter, since the pigeon came in from the sea." Mr. Hardy said. "We'll do our best to find the spot."

Mr. Ghapur leaned forward in his chair. "Nothing must happen to Tava. He is like one of my own family. When he was just a small child, I was the guest of Satish Nayyar." Turning to Mr. Delhi, he asked, "Do you remember the cheetah hunt?"

"I certainly do," Mr. Delhi recalled, "and my cousin will never forget how you saved Tava's life, at peril of your own, when the boy was attacked by the cheetah."

"It was a great honor," Ghapur said quietly. He turned back to Fenton Hardy and concluded, "I guess we've finished our mission here. Mr. Delhi will return with me to my home in Washington. His enemies must not know where he is, so we will leave the way we came. We are deeply grateful to you all."

"We'll try to justify your gratitude," Fenton Hardy promised.

Mr. Delhi asked that they spare no expense in tracing down every possible clue. "Incidentally," he added, "Tava brought along his favorite goshawk on this trip. This might help you locate him."

When he and Rahmud Ghapur had left, Mr. Hardy said to his sons, "I believe there's a connection between Tava's kidnappers, the rubies on the pigeon, and the smugglers of aliens from India. You boys made a start checking the coastline for clues. You might follow up on that, as well as try to locate the carrier pigeons' cote while I'm away. I'm due back in Washington tomorrow."

"We'll keep after the waterfront angle," Frank assured him. "We're going to do some sleuthing from the air, too, to track down the pigeon's owner."

The family was up early the next morning so that Fenton Hardy could catch the first plane to Washington. While the boys were feeding and watering the falcon, their mother brought them two hundred dollars cash and asked that they deposit it in the bank before three o'clock. They drove their father to the airport, then looked for their friend George Simons, who owned a helicopter.

"No passengers ahead of us today, I hope," said Frank.

"You're the first. Climb in. What are you fellows chasing this time?" the pilot asked with a smile.

"Carrier pigeons and their home cotes," Frank told him.

First they flew to the end of the bay and from

there headed in the southwesterly direction which the two carrier pigeons had followed. The pilot kept the helicopter at low speed while Frank scanned the land below.

Meanwhile, Joe was watching the horizon behind them for any slow-moving boat that might be plying between some ship and the shore. He saw none but suddenly cried out:

"Here comes a pigeon northeast of us!"

Simons held the helicopter stationary until the bird had come alongside and moved ahead of his craft. Then he trailed it. For about eight miles the pilot kept the pigeon in sight while Frank plotted its course on a map he had brought. Then, suddenly, the bird made a dive for a sparsely wooded area.

Simons stopped his forward flight and lowered the helicopter to get a better look. The boys carefully scrutinized the area, but there was no sign of a house or barn with a cote. Frank and Joe were puzzled, but finally concluded it must have been a wild bird that had just happened to take the southwesterly route.

Although the Hardys spent most of the morning scouting the Bayport environs, they saw no other pigeons.

At the airport, as the boys climbed into their convertible, Joe asked, "Where do we go from here?"

"We ought to go to the bank," his brother replied, starting the motor. "But let's scout around the waterfront first for the heavy-set, sun-tanned man wearing a ruby ring."

Joe nodded. "How about looking for that suspicious sailor on the *Daisy K?* If he's the fellow, he may be wearing the ring now."

They parked their car a block from the shoreline, then walked briskly to the dock area, where fishing boats, excursion steamers, deep-sea charter cruisers, and pleasure craft tied up. As the two headed for the *Daisy K,* Joe gripped Frank's arm and pointed toward an outdoor lunch stand.

"Look at the ring on that fellow on the second stool!" he said excitedly.

A stocky, dark-skinned sailor sat there eating. As he lifted a hamburger to his mouth, the sun sparkled on a ruby ring—the same unusual ring the falcon snatcher had been wearing!

The boys passed quickly and ducked behind a building.

"What'll we do now?" Joe asked.

"Let's confront him and see how he reacts," Frank urged. "We'll move in on either side."

"Okay."

They took seats next to the man and Frank looked him straight in the eye. "What did you want with our falcon?" he asked.

The man looked up, startled. "Falcon? You've mistaken me for someone else," he mumbled and backed off the stool.

"Let's confront him and see how he reacts,"
Frank urged

Joe gripped him by the shoulder. "If you won't tell us, you can explain it to the police!"

"The police? Say, what's going on? I don't know anything about a falcon, I swear!" The sailor's voice grew loud and he shook off Joe's hand.

"Where did you get that ruby ring?" Frank broke in, stepping in front of the suspect.

This question brought a curious reaction. Apparently the man thought the boys intended to steal it, for he yelled, "Oh, no, you don't!" and plunged headlong at Frank, trying to move past him.

Frank thrust out a leg in front of the sailor, who tripped over it and fell. Instantly Joe came down on his back, pinning him to the ground.

"Now maybe we'll get an answer!" he said.

CHAPTER VI

A Big Boner

BYSTANDERS had gathered around the Hardy boys and the sailor.

"All right, talk!" Frank ordered, dragging the man to his feet.

The heavy-set, dark-skinned sailor straightened up. Glaring at the Hardys, he asked, "What do you want to know about my ruby ring?"

"Where did you get it?" Joe asked.

"Well, I didn't steal it, if that's what you think," the man said sullenly. "I bought it from another sailor just last night."

"What did this man look like?" Frank pressed.

The sailor suddenly reddened. "Why—er—I don't know, but he also was Indian. Say, I can prove everything I told you!"

Turning, he yelled to the counterman to verify his story. To the Hardys' chagrin the counterman did so, saying he had seen the transaction.

"We're sure sorry," Frank apologized. "We—we made a mistake. We'd like to make up for it."

The sailor grinned. "Well, all right, you can pay my lunch check," he said. "I'm broke."

"Maybe we can do even better," Joe said. "Want to sell the ring?" he asked, recalling that Mr. Delhi had said to spare no expense in following up clues.

The sailor hesitated, then took off the ring, named the price he had paid for it, and said he would sell for a small profit. Frank paid him, as well as the lunch check, from his mother's two hundred dollars. The sailor saluted crisply and hurried away.

Shaking their heads ruefully, the Hardys resolved to be less hasty in jumping to conclusions. They went to the bank to deposit Mrs. Hardy's remaining bills, then continued on toward the dock where the *Daisy K* tied up. She was not in port.

"As long as we're here," said Joe, "we may as well make some inquiries about the crew."

They quizzed supply men and ships' captains. Finally one of the captains declared:

"That sounds like a fellow named Ragu, first mate on the *Daisy K*. Heavy-set. Piercing black eyes. Came from India. I've seen a ruby ring on him."

Frank and Joe could hardly believe their good fortune. That sailor they had seen leaning on the boat's rail must have been the original owner of the ring! The captain said he had just seen him in the Sea Foam Restaurant. The boys hurried there and spotted Ragu at a table in the far corner.

As the Hardys approached, Ragu glanced up and half rose from his chair, then slowly settled back.

"You're Ragu, aren't you?" Joe asked.

"Of what importance is that to you?"

"We'd like to know something about a ruby ring you've been wearing," Frank told him.

"I own no ring," the sailor said belligerently.

Frank displayed the ring he had just bought. "You don't own this ring now," he said evenly, "but you did. Where did you get it?"

Ragu snatched the ring and hurled it away.

"You are evil boys!" he almost screamed.

Instinctively Frank and Joe turned to recover the ring. Frank picked it up. When the boys whirled back, Ragu was dashing out a side door.

The Hardys started after him, but suddenly Frank stopped and said, "Joe, let him go. I'm sure that Ragu's the fellow who grabbed the falcon from you. If he doesn't think we're after him, and if he's connected with the senders of those rubies, maybe he'll lead us to them."

"Guess you're right, Frank."

They went back to their convertible. As Frank was about to pull away from the curb, a vivacious voice said:

"What a beautiful ring you're wearing, Frank."

Frank and Joe looked up into the smiling face of Callie Shaw, a close friend of Iola's. Blond, quick-witted, and carefree, she appealed particularly to Frank. Although interested, and frequently very helpful in the boys' sleuthing, the pretty brown-eyed girl loved to tease the Hardys.

"Is the ring a gift?" Callie asked.

"No," Frank replied with a smile. "It's a clue in a new case we've taken on."

Iola Morton had joined the group now and was talking to Joe. She said gaily, "Don't forget the fish fry at the farm this afternoon."

"Wouldn't miss it for all the mysteries in Bayport," Joe replied.

"The whole gang will be there," Iola said. "Why not bring along your hawk and give us a demonstration?"

"Sure thing!" Frank agreed.

"Be there about three," Callie said. "Games first and we'll eat at five."

The girls waved good-by and headed for a waterfront fish shop.

"If we're going to exhibit Miss Peregrine," said Joe, "we'd better go home and groom her!"

When they reached the house, the boys showed their mother the ring and told her how they had paid for it. "Mr. Delhi will reimburse us," Frank explained. "I'll put the ring in Dad's safe."

After lunch he and Joe fixed a bath for the falcon. Then they changed their clothes, picked up the bird, perch, bells and lure, and set off for the Morton farm. They found a lively gathering of a dozen couples playing spirited games of softball and badminton.

But the moment the young people saw the falcon, they focused all their attention on the bird. Joe set the perch on the ground and said they would let her fly later. The hawk remained quiet as he and Frank joined in the games.

Finally Chet, who was wearing a flashy dark-green shirt splotched with brown and white, said, "Show them what Miss Peregrine can do, fellows."

Frank looked around for a quarry. Suddenly a jay flew across the field at the edge of a woods. Frank picked up the hawk, yanked off the hood and flung the hawk in its direction. As the guests excitedly watched her fly toward the jay, a short-winged goshawk came rifling in from the woods and dived toward the jay.

"That's a trained bird!" Frank exclaimed.

Instantly the two hawks began to fight over the jay. Joe started forward, calling excitedly to the falcon. Frank held him back, saying:

"It's too late now. They'll fight to the death."

But the falcon abruptly shifted to avoid the vicious talons of the goshawk and then climbed up where she would have the advantage. While the hawks were maneuvering for position, the jay disappeared in the brush.

Frank and Joe whistled and shouted to Miss Peregrine, hoping to stop the fight. Suddenly the goshawk took flight and disappeared into the shelter of the woods. The falcon oriented herself, located the boys by the sound of their voices, and came down obediently to the feathered lure.

"Hey! You're pretty good!" Chet exclaimed admiringly, and the other young people applauded.

The Hardys smiled, relieved that their falcon was safe, then looked inquiringly toward the woods into which the goshawk had vanished.

"Come on, Joe and Chet!" Frank urged. "Let's find the owner of the hawk! It could be Tava."

Frank hooded the peregrine and placed her on her perch. Then the three boys hurried into the woods.

Joe spotted a trail of recently trampled grass. Eagerly the trio followed it. They had gone only about a hundred yards when they were confronted by a large red sign with white lettering:

DANGEROUS AREA! KEEP OUT!

The boys were puzzled, especially Chet, who was well acquainted with the woods. "Gosh, I never saw that before," he said. "What's going on here?"

The land looked undisturbed. There were no signs of digging, tree-felling, or other hazardous operations.

Farther ahead the boys came across similar warning signs.

Frank turned to Chet. "What could make this a dangerous area?" he asked.

"I don't know," his puzzled friend replied. "Old Mr. Smith who owns these woods used to encourage the public to picnic here."

"If any big project were under way, everybody in Bayport would have heard about it," Frank remarked.

"Let's split up and see if we can find out what's going on," Joe suggested.

He and Chet searched a wide sweep on either side of the trail, while Frank followed the trampled path. The boys lost sight of each other as the foliage became more dense. But Frank could check the others' positions from the sounds of their passage through the undergrowth. Soon these sounds were muffled, and the woods became a silent, twilight world.

Suddenly from Chet's direction came a cry for help.

"Chet's in trouble!" Frank yelled.

Instantly he and Joe were crashing through the underbrush to their friend's aid.

CHAPTER VII

Dangerous Explorations

For several anxious moments Frank and Joe could not locate Chet. But finally they came upon him huddled in a clump of brush near a brook.

"He's unconscious!" gasped Joe.

They knelt beside Chet, then carefully carried their friend out of the thicket to a clearing. As the boys gently placed him on the ground, they noticed blood oozing from a wound near the back of his head.

"This was no accident," Frank declared.

"Someone gave him a heavy blow!"

Both boys glanced around cautiously to make sure none of them was in immediate danger, then they gave Chet first aid. As Joe chafed the boy's wrists, Frank started for the brook to soak a handkerchief to bathe Chet's wound and brow.

He had gone only a few feet when he heard a

slight rustling sound. Looking around quickly, Frank spotted a movement in some bushes about fifty feet away. Without turning, he whispered:

"Joe, take care of Chet. I see someone. I'll be back as soon as I can."

Frank headed for the bushes, but almost at the same moment, someone went crashing through the underbrush. The young detective increased his own pace, following the fugitive by the sounds of flight.

Several hundred yards farther on, Frank spotted the back of a tall, thin man for a fleeting second.

Frank put on a burst of speed which brought him closer to the man. They were both making considerable noise now, as twigs and leaves crackled under their feet. For this reason Frank was not immediately aware of footsteps behind him. When he heard them, the boy started to turn, but the next second a heavy blow caught him on the side of his head. Knees buckling, Frank pitched forward and blacked out!

Back at the clearing, Joe had heard the sounds of the chase, but he was confident that his brother would be more than a match for any adversary. Then he went to the brook, soaked his handkerchief in the cool water, and bathed Chet's wound. The boy's eyes flickered open and he looked up dazedly.

"Take it easy," Joe advised. "Someone knocked you out. But Frank's after him now."

"I remember. Someone rushed up behind me and I yelled for help. He conked me." Chet relaxed and closed his eyes.

Joe sat down on a log to wait for Frank's return. Glimpsing the sky through the trees, he could see that the afternoon was waning. It struck him that their friends at the fish fry probably were wondering about the boys' long absence. Should he try to get Chet back and not wait for Frank? But Joe decided against this.

"Chet should take it easy," he thought.

As time passed and his brother still did not return, Joe grew worried. "Chet, I'd better look for Frank," he said. "Do you think you can make it back to the farm alone?"

"Guess so."

Joe helped him to his feet. The stout boy took a few steps, then stopped, admitting that he felt dizzy.

"You better rest a while longer," Joe said.

He rummaged in the undergrowth and found a strong, heavy stick. Handing it to Chet, he said, "You ought to be able to defend yourself with this. I'm going to hunt for Frank."

"Okay. I'll wait here."

Joe moved off into the woods, trying to follow the general direction Frank had taken. Several times he gave the Hardys' secret birdcall whistle, and listened eagerly for his brother's response. But it never came.

Joe trudged on, following the trail of trampled grass he had found. As he reached a dense section, he heard someone moving just ahead of him. Joe stopped and gave the whistle again. There was no reply, but the rustling grew louder. He looked about for a weapon, found a heavy stick, picked it up, and went forward.

As Joe crept around the bole of a large tree, he saw Frank staggering along!

"Frank, you've been hurt!" Joe cried. He gripped his brother around the shoulders and gently lowered him to the ground. As Frank looked up at him, Joe noticed that his brother was clutching a small pouch.

"Where did you get this?" Joe asked.

Frank blinked, looked down at the pouch as if seeing it for the first time, and muttered, "Don't know. Maybe the fellow who attacked me dropped it. Guess I picked it up." He sank back, exhausted.

Joe opened the small pouch and saw that it contained several reddish-brown nuts. He had never seen any like them and concluded they might be a good clue to the identity of the boys' assailant.

Right now, Joe faced a dilemma. Should he go for help and leave Frank and Chet? But he discarded the idea at once. Their enemy might return. He had to get both boys away as soon as possible!

"Suppose you rest for a few minutes, Frank," he suggested. "Then we'll take off."

Frank closed his eyes. He opened them ten minutes later, declaring he felt much better. Joe was seated beside him, gazing at the pouch.

"It's possible that we're close to the smugglers' hideout, Frank," he remarked.

A few minutes later Frank said that he felt strong enough to start back. Joe helped him up, and they moved off slowly in the lengthening shadows toward the spot where Chet waited. Because of the dusk and the condition of the two boys, further sleuthing was out of the question for the time being.

'But we'll pick up the trail first thing in the morning," Frank said with determination.

As they walked on, they discussed their experiences of the afternoon. When they reached the spot where Joe had left Chet, the Hardys did not see him.

"I hope he wasn't attacked again," Joe cried out.

"No such thing," came a voice so close to them that the Hardys jumped.

The next instant, Chet's perspiring head emerged from his splotched dark-green shirt, which blended well with the underbrush. The stout boy got up from his hiding place, grinning.

Frank and Joe roared with laughter. As their mirth subsided, Chet explained that he had felt too weak to fight anyone, even with the clublike stick Joe had given him. When he thought someone was coming, he had ducked into the bushes and put the shirt over his head as camouflage.

"But I guess it was my imagination," he said. "Haven't heard a thing since. Let's go!"

The boys made their way back to the trail and headed for the Morton farm. All the young guests had left except Callie. She and Iola were seated with Mr. and Mrs. Morton near the falcon's perch, keeping a close watch on the valuable bird.

At sight of Chet and Frank, the whole group ran forward. Mr. Morton asked, "What happened?"

"Got banged up a bit," Chet replied. "But there's nothing wrong with us that some food and a night's sleep won't cure."

"You bet," Frank spoke up, also trying to make light of their ordeal. "Anything left from the fish fry?"

"Come and get it!" Iola said.

While they were eating, the boys told the others of their strange experiences in the woods. Chet's father said that he would try to find out if Mr. Smith had posted the warning signs and why.

"Tomorrow we'll go back and investigate the place, anyway," Joe declared.

The Mortons and Callie begged the boys to be on their guard.

The following day was a cold and dreary one

for August, but after breakfast Frank declared he felt well enough to further investigate the woods near the Morton farm. He proposed that they take Ahmed along on their exploration.

"If we do run into a group of Indians, his knowledge will come in mighty handy."

Joe agreed. "I'll phone him. You get the car."

Ahmed, amazed to hear about the incident with the goshawk and the attacks on the boys, was eager to go. The boys asked Mrs. Hardy to keep an eye on the falcon, then set off in the convertible to pick up Ahmed at his bungalow. The rug dealer was hardly seated when he said tensely:

"If you have really found the hideout of these despicable smugglers and can bring them to justice, India will never be able to repay you."

Remembering the small pouch he had found in the woods, Frank pulled it out of his pocket and handed it to Ahmed. "I picked this up in the woods yesterday. Do you think it might be a clue?"

Ahmed's eyes narrowed as he scrutinized the bag and its contents. Then he said cryptically, "I believe this is indeed a clue in your search. These are betel nuts. Only lower-caste Indians chew them." Ahmed turned to Frank. "The person who attacked you and your friend may be one of the smuggled men or a servant to an Indian of wealth."

The Hardys looked at each other. The kidnapped Tava, perhaps? He was indeed one of great wealth. They wondered whether to tell Ahmed of Tava's disappearance, but decided not to do so unless it became necessary. "At least we should ask Mr. Delhi's permission first," they reflected.

A short time later Frank turned the car into the Morton driveway and Chet joined them at the barn. The foursome set out for the woods, taking a different route from the trail they had followed the previous day which Frank thought was closer. But a new obstacle presented itself—a long, impenetrable wall of vines and branches.

Ahmed paused and studied the barrier carefully. "These vines and branches," he said, "have been woven together by master craftsmen. Whoever had this constructed is indeed anxious to keep out strangers."

"I've never seen anything like it," said Frank. "Have you, Ahmed?"

"You have heard tales of the beaters who go out to stir up the tiger and the wild boar? They often use this weaving technique to make sure the animals will not escape while the hunter is moving in with his elephant, or the pig-sticker with his lance."

"What we need is a machete!" Joe remarked.

Ahmed and the three boys picked up stout pieces of fallen tree limbs and started to beat their way through. Now and then they stopped to listen for sounds that might indicate trouble. But apparently they were alone in the woods.

Presently a disturbing thought came to Frank. "It looks," he said, "as though we may have frightened our attackers away from the woods permanently."

Joe nodded but made no comment. Finally the searchers broke through the thick mesh of vines, spotted a fairly well-marked trail, and went ahead.

They walked for some time, searching carefully for clues, but saw nothing suspicious. Presently the foliage began to thin out. Frank held up a hand for silence. Then, dropping to his knees, he crawled forward.

"There's a hunting lodge ahead," he whispered. "And smoke is coming from the chimney."

Chet explained that Mr. Smith had built the lodge to entertain his friends during the hunting season, but that he never used it in the summer.

For several minutes Ahmed and the boys observed the lodge. Then Frank said:

"It looks deserted, though someone must have built a fire recently. Let's see what we can find out. But be careful!"

Did the lodge conceal dangerous smugglers—or the kidnappers? the Hardys wondered.

CHAPTER VIII

A Strange Lead

THE searchers warily circled the hunting lodge, but they came upon no one, nor was there any sign of activity inside. Still cautious, however, Frank whispered:

"Keep an eye on me, will you, while I get close enough to look through the windows?"

Frank hurried forward, zigzagging so that he would be an elusive target. At last he reached a corner of the low, wide veranda which ran around three sides of the building. Crossing to a large window, he looked into a handsomely furnished living room with a log fire burning. The room was unoccupied.

Frank moved stealthily from window to window. There were several rooms in the lodge, all well furnished. The bedrooms and kitchen showed evidence of a hasty exit of several people. Dirty dishes were piled high in the sink, and bureau drawers were open.

Frank signaled to the others and they came forward. Moments later all were inside the lodge, looking for clues to the vanished occupants.

Joe, who was more interested in where the occupants had gone, went through the kitchen and out to the back yard. At the edge of the woods he discovered a spring which flowed into a small creek. In the muddy earth around it were a number of footprints.

"Hey, come here!" he called. Ahmed, Frank, and Chet joined him. "Let's see where these tracks go."

"And look!" cried Chet, pointing in turn to several bright-red splotches on the ground.

"Looks like blood!" Joe exclaimed.

"Dried blood would be dark," Frank said. "That is brilliant red."

"This is a real clue," said Ahmed. "A user of betel nuts spits a bright-red fluid."

Their hopes raised by these latest discoveries, the searchers dashed into the woods, following the footprints Joe had discovered. When that trail ended, the boys spotted crushed leaves and broken twigs that marked the recent flight of several people. Red splotches made by the betel-nut user were here and there.

The foursome followed the trail to the edge of a rock-filled brook. There it was lost. Frank and Joe knelt at various points along the opposite bank, looking for some sign to indicate where the fleeing group had come out. But they found nothing and concluded that the fugitives had gone far downstream.

Convinced that there was no way of picking up the trail beyond the stream, Frank suggested that they all return to the lodge and try to find some clues to the occupants' identities.

In the rambling log structure each of the quartet took one of the bedrooms. There were visible fingerprints everywhere but not one clear set.

Suddenly Ahmed called out, "In here, boys! Look what I've found."

The others ran to a bedroom which was furnished more luxuriously than the others. Ahmed was holding a dark-brown object the size of a robin's egg. It looked like a salt shaker, was delicately carved, and had a number of colored bands for decoration. The initials T.N. were engraved on the bottom.

"What is it?" Frank asked, puzzled.

"A sandalwood scent box," Ahmed replied slowly.

"And the initials could stand for Tava Nayyar!" Frank cried.

"This must have been his 'prison'!" Joe said.

Frank nodded, then said, "I guess now we'd better tell the others about Tava."

Completely astounded, Ahmed and Chet listened to the story of the kidnapped Indian and the Hardys' suspicion that he had been held here.

"But where have they taken him?" Chet asked.

"Wherever Tava's been taken," said Frank, "you can be sure the place won't be so easy to find as this one was. His captors will see to that and will make it dangerous for anyone trying to find him."

"Then what's next?" Chet asked.

"I guess we'd better follow up the pigeon angle for further clues," Frank replied as all of them sat down to rest before starting back through the forest. "I haven't seen any signs of cotes around here. I thought for a while that maybe pigeons were kept here, both as food for the goshawk and as carriers for the smugglers. But I guess that the pet goshawk was given other food."

Chet sighed, "Let's go home. I'm hungry." He went into the kitchen, helped himself to a box of crackers, and passed them around.

Both Frank and Joe felt that the lodge and grounds should be guarded, in case Tava's kidnappers returned. As soon as they reached Chet's home they would phone Mr. Hardy's operative, Sam Radley, to take on this job.

Radley and the boys worked closely together. He admired Frank and Joe's sleuthing abilities, and encouraged them in every way he could.

Feeling rested, Ahmed and the boys started back through the forest. Several hundred paces later Frank spied a movement in the bushes and halted his companions.

"Who's there?" Frank called out.

No response. When he repeated his call, a boy about twelve years old stepped into the open.

"It's me, Gene Moran," the youngster said.

Relieved, the three sleuths pushed forward to meet the boy, who lived near the Hardys. Joe asked what he was doing in the woods.

"Looking for tree toads for my Boy Scout merit badge," Gene replied.

Chet grinned. "Find any?"

"Sure, a whole pocketful," the boy said, laughing.

"By the way," Frank put in, "did you see anyone else in these woods today besides us?"

"Yes, a bunch of dark-skinned people. They looked sort of like your friend." Gene bobbed his head at Ahmed.

"Where?"

Gene pointed in a southwesterly direction. "They were in a big hurry. Say, one fellow— about the same age as you, Frank—had a pet bird on his right wrist. And it had a funny cap pulled over its head."

"Were any of the people wearing foreign clothing?" Joe queried.

"No. They all had on regular American suits."

"Did they have a leader?"

Gene thought for a moment. "Guess you'd call the lightest one the leader. He was tall and cruel-looking. Wore a cap like a ship's captain and a dark-blue coat. Bet he is a captain, because I heard one of the other men ask him, 'Cap, got the stones?' "

Stones! Frank's and Joe's eyes flashed. Elated, they thanked Gene for his information. The boy looked at them curiously. "You working on a case?"

"That's right." Joe winked at Frank. "We're after a couple of toads ourselves. Big ones."

Gene grinned. "Hope you catch 'em."

"And good luck on your merit badge," said Frank.

Once more the Hardys, Chet, and Ahmed headed for the Morton farm.

"One thing I don't understand," said Chet. "Why didn't Tava escape yesterday when he was evidently within sight of us?" Chet asked.

Joe suggested that perhaps the youth was not being held against his will.

"It could be," said Frank, "that he has been given some phony story, believes it, and isn't even trying to get away!"

When they arrived at Chet's house, Frank telephoned Sam Radley. He related all the happenings in the woods and described the location of the hunting lodge. Mr. Hardy's operative assured him that he would start guarding the place at once.

"But I doubt that those people will return," he said.

Iola insisted that the Hardys and Ahmed stay for lunch.

"We don't need a second invitation," Joe said with a grin.

When the meal was over, the Hardys drove Ahmed home. They thanked the rug dealer for his help. He bowed politely and replied:

"It is you who are helping my friend Gaphur and my people. I shall be forever grateful to you."

Frank and Joe waved good-by, and the convertible moved away. As Frank turned into the Hardy driveway, Joe declared, "Boy, am I tired and hot! A shower will feel good!"

"That goes for me, too," Frank admitted. "About the liveliest thing I'm going to do the rest of today is make up a list of pigeon fanciers nearby and try to find out if one of them has lost any carrier pigeons recently."

Before locking the garage, they stopped to talk to the falcon. She was bobbing back and forth on her perch as though in welcome. Joe brushed his fingers along the bird's back between the shoulders and on the feathers of her wings.

"We sure deserted you today," he remarked.

After they had showered and put on clean clothes, Frank and Joe went to their father's study and started to check the classified telephone directory for pet shops.

"The owners ought to know something about pigeon fanciers," Joe declared.

They made a series of telephone calls which netted no information. There were only four listings left when Frank and Joe heard a noisy car coming down Elm Street.

"Sounds like Chet's jalopy," Joe said, getting up to look out a window. "And it is!" he added.

Usually the stout boy nursed along his prized possession as though it were made of solid gold. But today he was evidently in a hurry. He slammed on the brakes and rushed into the house and up the stairs so fast that he was out of breath for several moments.

"Hey, Chet, somebody chasing you?" Joe quipped.

Without replying, Chet held out his hand in which lay a capsule, similar to the one containing the rubies.

"Where did you get this?" Frank asked quickly.

Chet finally calmed down enough to speak. "I was standing outside the barn when I heard a plane. At the same time I spotted a pigeon overhead. Suddenly the pigeon flew directly toward the craft and crashed into its windshield."

"Wow!" Joe said. "That must have been the end of the poor bird."

"It was," Chet went on. "It plummeted right down into the middle of a field!"

"And you found it?" Frank queried.

Chet nodded. "This capsule was on its leg. Wait till you see what's in it!"

CHAPTER IX

A Harsh Skipper

ALTHOUGH Chet had opened the capsule when he had removed it from the pigeon, he would not reveal the contents to the Hardys. Instead, he waited as Frank removed the top.

Inside was a tightly rolled bit of paper.

Frank smoothed out the note. A message, printed in block letters, read:

CAUGHT L ABOUT TO SQUEAL. HOLDING HERE. NO DELIVERIES UNTIL REPLACEMENT ARRIVES.

Frank slapped Chet on the back. "Good work, pal. This may help to speed up our case."

As Chet beamed with pride, Frank turned to Joe. "I guess we'd better forget those pigeon fanciers for the time being and concentrate on this new clue."

"You bet!"

They examined the paper to see if it held any further clues. Holding it to the light, Frank studied the watermark. It looked like a fouled anchor insigne with several other figures that might be porpoises or sea horses.

"Look at this, fellows," he said. "The next step is to see if we can trace the origin of the paper."

From a list in Mr. Hardy's files, they selected the best-known paper manufacturers and called them asking if it belonged to a special customer.

They were told in each case that the company would check and let them know.

"Now all we can do is wait," Frank said.

The next day the boys stayed at home all morning, but no telephone calls came from the paper manufacturers. At lunchtime Joe said, "While we're waiting, let's investigate that man Gene Moran told us about yesterday—the one who might be a ship's captain."

"Okay. How about trying the Bayport waterfront again? Maybe the owner of that restaurant where we saw Ragu can give us a clue."

The Hardys drove to the docks and headed for the eating place. When they questioned the proprietor about a tall, cruel-looking sea captain, he grinned and shouted to two men who were busily eating steaks at a table in a far corner of the room.

"These boys are looking for a tall, cruel-looking captain, men. Either one of you like to take the job?"

"What's it for?" asked one. Then laughing loudly, he said, "A high school play?"

Chagrined, the Hardys headed for the door. To their amazement they heard the restaurant man remark, "The Hardy boys. Their pop's a big-time detective."

"Hey, Zeke! We'll have to watch our step!"

Raucous laughter followed as the boys left. They visited other spots along the waterfront but saw no likely suspect. Finally they paused near a small fishing craft. A jovial-looking man called down to them from the upper deck:

"Are you the lads who are huntin' for a cruel-lookin' skipper?"

"How'd you hear about it?" asked Joe.

"Joke's all up and down the waterfront," the man told them. "Just the same, if I was lookin' for a fellow of that stripe, I'd check with Captain Flont of the *Daisy K*."

The *Daisy K* again, the Hardys thought excitedly.

"Was Captain Flont's boat out at sea yesterday?" Frank queried.

"No. She was tied to her bollards all day. I can swear to that, since I didn't leave port either."

"Was the captain aboard the *Daisy K*?" Joe asked.

"Not until late in the evening."

The Hardys thanked the man and hurried to the anchorage of the *Daisy K*. As they drew closer, they spotted Captain Flont in the deckhouse. Ragu was lounging on the rear deck.

Frank and Joe halted at the gangway, and with nautical courtesy, Frank called, "Ahoy, the *Daisy K.* May we come aboard?"

Captain Flont leaned out the window and said harshly, "If you've got business with us, come aboard. But make it snappy!"

When the boys stepped onto the deck, Ragu looked up with an insolent stare. They peered at him intently in return, but the mate did not flinch.

As Captain Flont approached the Hardys, Frank decided that the best way to obtain information was through a ruse. Choosing his words carefully, he said, "We're trying to locate a couple of our friends who were going fishing with you yesterday."

"We didn't go fishing yesterday," Captain Flont replied quickly.

"Oh, then maybe you were the captain who was in Smith's woods yesterday," Joe broke in.

Flont scowled. "I wasn't in any woods. Now get off this ship!"

The Hardys held their ground. "How about your man Ragu?" Frank asked. "Was he there?"

At this, Ragu stalked up behind them. "I was with Captain Flont yesterday," he growled. "We were on ship's business."

"Now you have your answers," the skipper shouted. "Get off my ship!"

Frank and Joe did not move quickly enough to

suit the captain. His shout had aroused the other two crew members, who came up from below. They gripped the unwanted callers by the elbows and rushed them off the vessel. The boys were thrown forcibly onto the dock.

As the sailors returned to the gangplank, Frank and Joe heard one of them mutter, "It's lucky they didn't show up for the moonlight ride!"

The Hardys brushed themselves off and walked back to their car. As Frank drove off he said wryly, "We found out one thing—those men sure don't want *us* around."

Joe nodded. "It's strange that it takes a captain, a mate, and two crew members to run a fifty-foot fishing cruiser. What do you think that fellow meant about a moonlight ride?"

"I don't know, but we ought to find out if he meant tonight. There'll be a full moon. Let's take the *Sleuth* out and keep an eye on the *Daisy K.*"

At home the boys found a telegram from one of the paper mills. Frank read it and said:

"Joe, did you ever hear of the Mediterranean Steamship Line? The records of this paper company show that the fouled anchor stationery was made for them and is used on all their ships. It was sold through the London office."

Joe said he had never heard of the line, but went to one of his father's bookcases and brought back a book containing ships' registries. He thumbed through it, then stopped at one page.

"Here it is," he announced. "Some of their ships ply between New York and the Middle East. I'll check recent arrivals and departures."

"Good idea."

As Joe scanned the shipping news in the *Bayport Times,* he said, "Here's an item on one—the *Continental.* She arrived in New York early this week. Her normal course would have taken her close to the coast at Bayport. Say, do you think the *Continental* might be the ship that's bringing aliens to the United States?"

"Could be," Frank said. "But it might just be a ship on which one of the gang was traveling."

Determined to track down every possible clue, Frank called the Mediterranean Line's New York office. He explained that the Hardys were detectives, working on a government case, and asked for a list of Indian passengers on recent voyages to New York. The passenger agent assured him that it would be mailed at once, together with any other helpful information the line could give.

"With that cooperation, it sounds as if the company's on the up and up," Frank remarked.

Just as the moon was rising that evening, Frank and Joe headed for the *Sleuth,* which was still moored at the dock they had left it the night of the fire. They paused to note the progress of repairs on their boathouse.

"It'll be at least two weeks before we can take the *Sleuth* back," Frank commented.

The boys were thrown onto the dock

"Yes, and the firebug hasn't been caught yet," Joe said as Frank took the wheel.

Soon they were speeding out of Bayport harbor. There were a number of islands near the inlet where they could wait for their quarry. Frank chose one that lay in shadows, cut the motor, and turned off their running lights.

"I feel like one of those falcons 'waiting on' until its prey comes along," Joe said, grinning.

In the moonlight the boys could see boats moving up and down the harbor, but all of them were pleasure craft. Finally, however, Frank whispered:

"There's a boat with the *Daisy K*'s lines."

Both boys positively identified Captain Flont's craft as it chugged past them. They gave it a reasonable lead, then started after it. The chase continued for about five miles, then the *Daisy K* slowed down. Frank cut his engine.

A few minutes later a large motor dory appeared beyond the fishing boat and pulled alongside. A rope ladder clattered over the rail of Flont's ship and two men scrambled down the rungs into the dory.

As the smaller boat pulled away toward the open sea, the *Daisy K* started up again, turned in a wide arc, and headed back toward Bayport.

"We've *got* to find out where that dory's going!" Joe said.

The *Sleuth* took up the chase!

CHAPTER X

Hunting a Hawk

THE Hardys had been following the mysterious dory for some time when the *Sleuth*'s motor began to sputter and the craft lost way.

Joe, seated on the forward deck as lookout, whirled around and asked, "What's the matter?"

"Sounds as if we're out of gas," Frank replied.

"Impossible," Joe said. "The gauge read full when I checked at the dock."

Frank unscrewed the tank cap and beamed his flashlight inside. "I have news for you, Joe," he said. "It still reads full, but there isn't a drop of gas in the tank!"

The Hardys examined the gauge and discovered that it was jammed.

"This didn't jam by itself," Frank declared. "Someone tampered with it!"

"Someone from the *Daisy K!*" Joe guessed.

By this time the motor dory was out of sight. In disgust the boys brought out the emergency fuel can and emptied its contents into the tank. Since there was little hope now of locating the dory with their limited gas supply, the Hardys headed for home. While Frank fixed the gauge, they speculated about where the dory had come from. Perhaps from a ship waiting at sea? The boys could see no lights to indicate any vessel, however, and concluded that the dory might be planning to meet a passing ship later.

"I wonder who those two men were who climbed off the *Daisy K*," Frank said thoughtfully.

Joe shrugged. "I guess our only hope of solving that is to keep the *Daisy K*'s crew under close observation," he commented. "When we get back to town, let's ask one of Dad's operatives to watch them."

"Jeff Kane's in town," Frank suggested.

When the boys reached Bayport, Frank telephoned the detective. Kane readily agreed to take over the assignment.

Early the next morning, after feeding the falcon, the boys took turns phoning the pet shops which they had not had time to call the day before. This time they were more successful. Two of the owners supplied them with the names of carrier pigeon fanciers. Some of these were in Bayport, while the others were a distance away.

With Frank at the wheel of the convertible, the Hardys started on their quest. The first place was only a half mile from their home. The pigeon keeper, a young man about twenty-five, proved to be a squab breeder who kept a few carrier pigeons as a hobby. He showed them to Frank and Joe.

"I enter these in cross-country races," he said. "My birds have brought me several cups and ribbons," he added, stroking one of the racers fondly.

In reply to a question from Frank, the young man said he had never taken his birds out on the water and released them.

"In fact, I don't know anyone around here who would have reason to," he said, "because the contests are always from inland cities to the coast."

The Hardys thanked him for the information and went on their way. Both of the other local men proved to be above suspicion as well.

The next name on their list was Reed Newton, who lived five miles away. When Frank and Joe reached his home, they found him to be a retired carpenter in late middle age, who had flown pigeons as a hobby for many years. He had a large cote and several breeding cages.

"You raise more pigeons than you train and fly, don't you, Mr. Newton?" Frank asked.

"Oh, yes," the fancier replied. "I sell them." He smiled boyishly. "I may sound a bit vain, but my pigeons are becoming known all over the world."

"Has anyone purchased a large number of birds from you recently?"

Reed Newton wrinkled his brow for some moments, then replied, "Not recently. But about two years ago I had a big order. A young man from India, named Bhagnav, bought a whole flock of pigeons."

"Bhagnav!" Joe exclaimed, but recovered quickly and added, "That's an unusual name."

"Can you describe this man?" Frank asked.

"Well, as I remember, he was a tall, slender, rather handsome fellow of about twenty-five. One thing I particularly remember was a scar at the base of his chin. It stood out clearly because it was a slightly lighter shade than the rest of his face."

Frank and Joe could hardly believe their good fortune in picking up this clue. Was the Bhagnav who had purchased the pigeons related to the Indian government official who was now using the name of Delhi?

After the Hardys had left Mr. Newton, they speculated about the man named Bhagnav who had bought the pigeons.

"It's possible," said Frank, "that he was an impostor who had planned this smuggling racket as far back as two years ago."

"Right. Figuring that if anyone uncovered the plot, the real Bhagnav would be blamed. We must phone Mr. Delhi about this as soon as we get home."

The drive to the farm of John Fenwick, the

last pigeon fancier on the boys' list, was long. On the way they stopped at a roadside restaurant to have lunch.

When Joe spotted a sign with the name FEN-WICK at the foot of a lane, he exclaimed:

"What a weird setup for a pigeon fancier!"

On the lawn inside the cyclone fence that lined the property were several perches. Each of them held a hooded hawk!

"Fenwick must be breeding fighter pigeons!" Frank grinned as he turned into the drive.

A pleasant-looking man in his middle thirties strode briskly from the back yard. He was dressed in rough clothing, had on a tight-fitting cap, and held two coils of nylon rope over his arm.

"We're looking for John Fenwick," Frank announced.

"That's me," the man said with a smile.

"We're interested in your pigeons," Joe said.

Mr. Fenwick laughed and remarked, "You're about two years too late for that. As you can see from the perches on the lawn, I've switched my interest to falconry."

"We have a peregrine falcon," Joe replied. "That's the reason we came to talk to you. Our falcon brought down a pigeon and we were trying to find the owner so we could settle accounts."

"Fine attitude, son," Mr. Fenwick declared. "Since you're interested in the birds yourself, you might like to come along with me today. I'm going to Cliff Mountain to get a young hawk from an eyrie—that's a nest—I've been observing."

Frank and Joe were thrilled at this idea. Frank suggested that Mr. Fenwick put his gear in their car and let them drive him to Cliff Mountain. He accepted, and as they drove along he explained that he was particularly interested in peregrines.

"I spotted one of their nests out on the mountain, and have been watching the tercel and the falcon. The eggs have been hatched now. There are four of them. I'll take only one young hawk out of the eyrie and leave the rest to fly away and raise broods of their own. The parent birds will return next year to nest again."

When he and the boys arrived at Cliff Mountain, Frank parked the car and Mr. Fenwick led the way up the trail to the precipice that had given the mountain its name. The going was rugged, but the boys' enthusiasm for hawking and adventure spurred them on.

When they reached the edge of the shaly cliff, Mr. Fenwick tied a heavy rope around a sturdy oak which seemed to be growing out of the rocks. The loose end was dropped over the side of the cliff, its entire one hundred and twenty-five feet hanging down.

"Usually," Mr. Fenwick explained, "it's a good idea to have a rope that will reach all the way to the bottom of the cliff. Then, if you can't climb back to the top safely, you can at least get to the ground without injury. But this cliff is too high for that. No alternative but to come back up."

Mr. Fenwick went over the edge of the cliff. He lowered himself about sixty feet, then called to the boys:

"There are three fledglings. One egg didn't hatch."

The mother hawk was not in sight. But Mr. Fenwick wasn't taking any chances and called up again, "Keep your eyes open for the mother. She's likely to resist an invasion of her nest. I don't want any trouble, if I can help it. I've been attacked before and it's no fun."

In a few minues Mr. Fenwick announced that he had one of the young birds in his packsack and was coming up. He signaled to be lifted to the rim. As he came over the edge and the rest of the line was pulled up, Mr. Fenwick said:

"Funny, I haven't seen any sign of the tercel, either. Usually he'll do the hunting for food for the young. Then the falcon will take the quarry from him in mid-air, pluck it, and feed the fledglings."

"Do you think someone might have shot the tercel and the falcon is getting the food?" Frank asked.

"That's possible," Mr. Fenwick replied. "And she will have to do all the work herself until the young ones can fly."

Then the hawk hunter displayed the fledgling.

The falcon's tail and wing feathers were short because the bird was so young. Small tufts of down clung to them. The bird's feet were a light greenish gray instead of brilliant orange like the adults'.

Both Frank and Joe noticed how large the feet were. They were already fully grown, even though its feathers were still developing.

The thing that amazed them most was that the young falcon was brownish black instead of blackish blue like their own hawk. Mr. Fenwick explained that the young birds never have the same plumage color and markings as the adults.

"Next spring this bird will begin to molt—that is, drop her old feathers and grow new ones. Those will be adult plumage like your peregrine's."

"Is that true for all hawks?" Joe asked.

"Yes," Mr. Fenwick replied as he put the fledgling back in the pack to begin the return journey.

When they reached Mr. Fenwick's home, the falconer extended a cordial invitation to return soon.

Back at their own house, they found Sam Radley waiting. He was seated in the garden with Mrs. Hardy and Aunt Gertrude. The falcon sat on the perch beside them.

As Radley began his report, the two women arose and went into the house.

"No one returned to the hunting lodge and I

doubt that anyone will, since they'll figure it's being watched. But as I was leaving Smith's woods, I met Mr. Morton. He told me that Mr. Smith's lawyer informed him that the property was leased for the summer to a dark-skinned man by the name of Sutter. I have a feeling he's one of our Indian boys."

Frank and Joe agreed.

At that moment a special-delivery letter arrived for the boys from the Mediterranean Line. It stated that no Indians had arrived on any of their vessels' recent trips to New York.

"This information may interest you, however," the letter went on. "A couple of years ago there was an Indian member of the *Continental*'s crew named Bangalore. He jumped ship. This company is particularly disturbed, because the immigration authorities hold us responsible for such things."

As he folded the letter, Frank said, "I wonder if we could get a photograph of Bangalore."

"I'll try to locate one," Radley offered.

Frank then told him of the clue about the pigeon fancier using the name Bhagnav, and the boys' decision to phone Mr. Delhi. Joe put in a call, but there was no answer at Mr. Ghapur's home, where the emissary was staying.

"Anything more I can do for you boys?" Radley asked. "I'll continue to keep an eye on the lodge."

Frank and Joe could think of nothing else. They mentioned Kane's shadowing the *Daisy K's* crew and that they expected a report from him soon.

"And I think we should talk to the Coast Guard," Frank remarked.

"I did that while I was waiting for you," Radley said. "The local men have found nothing suspicious on boats or ships in the area they cover. Of course they don't go out far beyond the twelve-mile limit. Does that suggest anything to you?"

"You bet it does!" Joe spoke up. "For one thing, it seems to back up our idea that a large ship anchors offshore, receives some sort of signal —or maybe sends its own message by carrier pigeon. Then the smuggled Indians are taken off in boats like the motor dory we trailed last night."

"But why couldn't the Coast Guard fly out there and spot such a transfer?" Frank pointed out. "When the dory reaches our waters, it could be nabbed."

"I suppose they might," Radley agreed. "But if the smuggled Indians swam a distance from a large ship to the smaller boat at night, the Coast Guard sure would have trouble spotting them."

"And it's impossible for them to cover every bit of shore line at once," Frank added, "especially at night when a dory could slip in. It might even be that the aliens swim the last half mile."

After Radley left, Frank and Joe talked over

their next move. "I suggest that we use Miss Peregrine for a little sleuthing," Frank said.

"How?"

"Let's take the falcon out to the Morton farm and have George Simons meet us there with his copter. It's a shorter drive for us there than to the airport and maybe Chet would like to go along. We'll go up in the chopper and keep watch for a pigeon coming from the ocean and heading southwest. If we spot one, we'll follow it until the bird starts down to its cote. Then we'll turn the falcon loose and let her trail the pigeon right to its cote. That way we ought to be able to intercept any message it may be carrying."

"You mean we'll kill two clues with one bird?" Joe grinned.

Frank first phoned Chet, who said, "Count me in. I sure would like to go along."

Then Frank called George Simons, who agreed to meet them at the farm in half an hour. Joe got the hawk's equipment, hooded and wristed her, and the boys drove off. When they reached the farm, the helicopter was already settling in an open area behind the barn. The boys headed for it to tell Simons their plan.

Chet, seeing them from the kitchen window, came outside and followed them. As he ambled past a corner of the barn, a masked figure moved up behind him. Chet's arms were pinned behind his back and a hand was clamped over his mouth!

In a low, fierce whisper, the masked man ordered, "Bring that falcon to your barn and leave it there. If you don't, you and the Hardys will be in serious trouble! And don't tell anyone why you're doing it!"

Desperately Chet squirmed and twisted in the grasp of his assailant but could not free himself!

CHAPTER XI

A Ruse

THE masked man tightened his grip.

"Listen, fat boy! Get that hawk if you value your life and the Hardys'!"

"All right," Chet finally said. "I'll do it."

The masked man pushed Chet along until they were close to a small door in the barn. Then he turned him loose and darted into the darkness of the barn, closing the door behind him.

Chet walked toward the Hardys with trembling legs. As Frank and Joe explained their plans to Simons, Chet interrupted, saying:

"Sounds swell. M-mind if I hold the f-falcon on the trip?"

"But the bird isn't accustomed to you," Frank said. "She wouldn't respond to your commands."

"Well, can't I at least h-hold her until you s-spot the pigeon?" Chet pleaded.

Frank and Joe exchanged puzzled glances.

They both sensed something was wrong with Chet, for he was not usually so nervous.

"That wouldn't work too well, either," Frank told him.

Chet cast an anxious glance over his shoulder in the direction of the barn, then stared at the hooded falcon. She was standing quietly on Joe's gauntlet. He was checking the jesses to make certain that they were firmly fastened to the bird's legs. Then he unsnapped the swivel hook, so that he could release the falcon quickly.

Suddenly Chet dived at Joe and grabbed for the bird! With a startled cry Joe stepped back and the falcon flapped her wings to hold her balance.

Frank clutched the stout boy's arm. "What's wrong with you, Chet? You act as though you're crazy! This bird can be ruined if she's disturbed. You mustn't make a pass at her like that! Move gently and slowly or she will bate off the hand."

Finally Chet decided the Hardys must be told about the threat. He glanced again at the barn, then said in a hoarse whisper:

"L-listen, fellows. A masked man stopped me at the barn a couple of minutes ago and ordered me to get the falcon from you. He told me to leave it inside the barn. If I don't, your lives and mine won't be worth a nickel!"

Simons, who had heard Chet's explanation, leaned out of the cockpit in amazement and said:

"Trouble! Can I help?"

Frank and Joe were grim, realizing that the only way out was through a ruse.

"You sure can," Frank told the pilot. "We'll give the hawk to Chet. He can take his time about getting it to the barn. In the meantime, Joe and I will pretend we've gone off with you in the copter, but we'll sneak out the other side, double back, and try to nab this guy and anyone who might be with him."

Joe helped Chet put the gauntlet on. Then he switched the falcon to the youth's wrist and handed him the end of the leash. In a loud voice he called "Good luck!" as though Chet had asked to borrow the hawk for an afternoon's hunting.

Simons jumped to the ground and the Hardys entered the passenger compartment. Then, while Chet and the pilot stood close together beside the helicopter to cut off any view from underneath the craft, Frank and Joe quickly slipped out the far side and took cover in back of some bushes. From there they made their way toward the barn as the copter rose and headed toward the woods.

Chet, who had started for the barn, was having trouble with the falcon. She bobbed up and down on his wrist, turned toward the throbbing sound of the rotors on the helicopter, and flew out to the end of the leash several times.

Chet, however, managed to get her to the barn. He rolled open the big door and placed the bird inside.

"Pretty rough on the hawk," Frank whispered to Joe. "But I guess Chet is scared plenty, too."

The frightened boy turned and hurried to the house. After he had climbed the rear steps and slammed the kitchen screen door behind him, the masked man slipped furtively out of the barn with the hawk under one arm.

Instantly the Hardys were upon him, and at a shrill whistle from Joe, Chet dashed back on the double. As Joe took the hawk, Frank pinned the prisoner to the ground and ripped off his mask.

Ragu! The first mate from the *Daisy K* stared insolently at the boys.

"Well," said Frank grimly as he let the sailor up but kept hold of him, "suppose you talk."

"You threatened me and the Hardys," Chet growled.

"That was just to make you get the hawk," Ragu answered. He watched Joe sullenly as he took the gauntlet from Chet and wristed the falcon.

"I know someone who will pay me well for a trained bird," Ragu went on.

"You'll have to give a better reason than that," Frank told him. "How did you know we would have the falcon out here?"

"I—I was hiding in your back yard this afternoon and overheard you making plans to bring the hawk here."

"Keep talking," said Joe.

"I've told you all I know," the sailor insisted.

"It will go easier with you if you tell the truth," Frank said. "What do you know about the smuggling and kidnapping rackets around here?"

Ragu winced but remained silent. Joe burst out, "I'm sure you can tell plenty about Captain Flont and the *Daisy K.*"

The sailor's muscles twitched nervously. "Let me go!" he shouted. "I don't know anything."

The boys marched the man to the kitchen porch. Frank and Joe kept a close watch on him while Chet went to phone Chief Collig.

"Tell him," Frank said, "that we have a prisoner for him. He can book Ragu for assault on you today and Joe the other day, and attempts to steal the falcon."

The group waited until they saw the Bayport patrol car turning into the Morton driveway. Then, with Frank and Chet holding the sailor firmly by the arms, they started toward the police car.

Chief Collig and Patrolman Smuff climbed out. As they eyed the hawk, Frank explained the circumstances of the capture, and told Smuff that Ragu was the thief they had been looking for.

Before Smuff or the chief had a chance to comment, Frank suddenly cried out:

"Joe, there's a pigeon! It's winging from the same direction as the other ones we've spotted. Let the hawk loose!"

Hearing this, Ragu began to cry out oaths in his native language. The Hardys were sure he must know that the pigeon was carrying a message or more rubies!

Joe unhooded the falcon. She spotted the pigeon, took off into the air, and climbed toward it.

"Chief, I'm sure Ragu is guilty of a lot more than he's admitting," Joe said.

"It seems that way," the officer said.

"We'll be in to prefer charges against him sometime tonight," Frank said.

"Good enough," Chief Collig agreed.

Smuff hustled Ragu into the patrol car and the three rode away.

The boys, shading their eyes, were following the flight of the bird. The peregrine and its prey had moved off over the wooded area and a moment later the pigeon was lost to view.

The Hardys' hearts sank. Had the bird escaped?

CHAPTER XII

Intercepted Ransom

"THE hawk mustn't lose that pigeon!" Joe cried.

As the boys watched tensely, the peregrine poised for a second, then dived like a miniature rocket. Frank, Joe, and Chet ran across the fields, their eyes still following the hawk.

Suddenly, through a rift in the trees, they could see both birds.

"The hawk's got it!" Frank exclaimed a moment later as the two birds dropped into the woods.

"Come on!" Joe shouted, starting to run.

When the boys did not immediately find the spot where the pigeon and the hawk had fallen, they spread out and searched the bushes for some time, but without success.

"Your falcon's got to be here some place," Chet said.

Just then they heard the whirring of the helicopter and hurried to a clearing, where they could spot the aircraft. They saw Simons beckon them to follow him.

The boys nodded and moved along the edge of the woods, guided by their friend in the sky. Presently he turned the craft and flew directly over the trees. Now Simons whirled up, then lowered quickly.

Frank interpreted the maneuver. "He's trying to tell us the birds are right around here."

Joe held out his gloved hand and whistled sharply. There was a movement in the brush a few yards ahead of the boys. Then they spotted the peregrine falcon and her quarry.

The younger Hardy moved in slowly and picked up the falcon and the mangled pigeon.

"This time she earned a meal," Joe said, spotting a telltale red container fastened to one of the pigeon's legs.

Frank removed the capsule and opened it. As he shook it gently, two rubies fell out.

"More of the ransom gems!" he declared.

Excitedly the trio ran toward the Morton farm. The helicopter was still hovering overhead when they came out into the clearing. Joe waved their thanks. Then the pilot headed for the airport to keep another appointment.

When Frank and Joe reached their car they said good-by to Chet and drove home. After putting the falcon in the garage and setting the burglar alarm, the boys went into the house. A message was waiting for them to phone Jeff Kane. He had shadowed the captain and crew members of the *Daisy K,* and had investigated their reputations, but could find nothing suspicious in their activities. He learned that Captain Flont ruled them with an iron hand and they seemed to fear him.

"If anything crooked is going on," Frank said to Joe, "it's well concealed, that's for sure."

Joe put through another call to Rahmud Ghapur, who answered at once. When he told Mr. Ghapur that the Hardys had two important pieces of information for Mr. Delhi, the importer asked that Joe not reveal them on the phone.

"I'll pass along your message to Mr. Delhi," Ghapur promised. "He'll probably want to fly up to Bayport sometime tonight."

"We'll be waiting for him."

The Indian arrived about eight o'clock, and he and the boys went to Mr. Hardy's study.

As Mr. Delhi settled himself in a chair, Frank unwrapped the two rubies and the ring, and explained how the Hardys had gotten them. Mr. Delhi examined them, then finally said:

"I could almost swear that these are some of the ransom rubies. This poses a serious problem."

He looked from one boy to the other and they felt that something had displeased him. "I do not want to seem ungrateful," Delhi said, "but if these are part of the ransom, and are not received by the fiends who are holding Tava, he may come to harm."

Frank and Joe were thunderstruck.

"I'm afraid we didn't realize that," Frank replied. "But we may be close enough to these kidnappers to catch them before they attempt anything drastic."

The Hardys told Delhi about the goshawk and the hunting lodge in the woods and the possible flight of Tava with his captors.

Then Frank showed him the sandalwood scent box that Ahmed had found at the lodge. Tenderly Delhi cupped the box in his hands.

"My friends," he said with emotion, "this box was given to Tava by his father at a ceremony I myself witnessed. May I keep it until Tava is found?"

"Of course," Frank replied.

Delhi asked, "You have someone watching this hunting lodge at all times?"

The Hardys reassured him on this point. Then they concluded with the story of the man who had purchased carrier pigeons from Mr. Newton under the name Bhagnav.

"My real name!" Delhi exclaimed. "But not one of my relatives has ever been in this country."

"We thought he was an impostor," Frank said.

"What does this man look like?" Delhi asked.

"We were told he is tall, slender, handsome—

about twenty-five years old. He has a prominent scar on his chin."

As the Indian weighed this information, his brow furrowed. Then he said, "The description sounds vaguely familiar. I shall speak to Rahmud Ghapur about this. Perhaps he will recognize the man. In any case, I'm sure the impostor is an enemy."

Joe changed the subject. "Does the name Ragu mean anything to you?" he asked.

Mr. Delhi thought this over, then said, "No. Can you describe him?" he asked.

But the description of a swarthy, short, heavy-set man did not help.

Frank said, "Ragu works here on a fishing boat called the *Daisy K*. Right now, though, he is in jail. We promised to go there tonight and prefer charges. Will you come with us and see if you know Ragu?"

"I shall be glad to go," he said. "But I suggest, in case we should be followed, that we try to throw off any pursuers."

Driving to police headquarters, Frank took every precaution to be sure that no one trailed them.

They learned, when they arrived, that Chief Collig was at home for a late dinner, but would return in a few minutes. The sergeant on duty assisted them in filing charges against Ragu. When the boys explained the reason for Mr.

Delhi's presence, he took the callers to the cell where Ragu was being held. On the way the sergeant said that the prisoner had been informed of his rights, had refused a lawyer, and had admitted nothing.

When Ragu saw the Hardys he stared at them balefully. He was about to say something, but suddenly his glance rested upon Mr. Delhi. A look of awe and fright spread over his face and he staggered backward.

"Mr. Bhagnav!" he cried.

Mr. Delhi gazed at the prisoner, then said to the boys, "I do not know this man, but apparently he recognizes me from newspaper photographs or public functions."

Following up the advantage of the prisoner's discomfiture, Frank asked him whether he was ready to talk. Ragu did not answer.

Just then Collig arrived. After the police chief was introduced to Mr. Bhagnav, the boys turned the ransom rubies over to the officer for safe-keeping.

When Ragu saw the gems he gasped but made no comment. The police chief ordered the jailer to unlock the cell door. They all went inside. Forming an arc about the prisoner, they began to question him.

Ragu remained defiant and uncooperative, but the Hardys felt he was almost frightened enough to make a full confession.

Chief Collig asked him to explain the reasons for the attempted thefts of the falcon and the threats to Chet and the Hardys, then added, "And tell us all you know about the operations of the *Daisy K.*"

Again the mention of Flont's ship had a visible effect on the first mate. Eyes wide, he stared at Chief Collig for a long moment. Then, abruptly, his shoulders sagged and he looked at the floor.

All further questions about Captain Flont or the *Daisy K* aroused no response.

Finally Mr. Delhi asked Ragu probing questions about the smuggling of aliens from India into the United States, and more particularly about the kidnapping of Tava Nayyar.

Ragu looked up, eyes flashing, and uttered one brief phrase in his native language. Mr. Delhi nodded, then turned to the others.

"Ragu wishes to talk to me alone," he said.

The boys and the police chief left the cell and waited at the end of the corridor.

Ten minutes later Mr. Delhi called, "It is settled."

When the others returned to the cell, Mr. Delhi said, "Ragu has convinced me that he knows little. But he is willing to tell us that much."

CHAPTER XIII

Attack in the Night

CHIEF Collig called in a police stenographer to take down Ragu's statement. As Mr. Delhi nodded to Ragu, the *Daisy K's* first mate began his story.

"First, I know nothing about any smuggling of my countrymen into the United States. I—I did join the group that was planning a kidnapping. But you must believe me—I did not know until too late who the victim was going to be."

"But you know that kidnapping is a criminal act!" the police chief said severely. "Just what was your part in it?"

"A very small one," Ragu insisted. "I ran errands. Once a man that came to our ship gave me a letter. He told me to deliver it to the Bayport Hotel."

"What was the name of the man who came to

the *Daisy K?*" Chief Collig broke in. "And what did he look like?"

"I do not know his name," Ragu said emphatically. "He was short, and had brown hair. The man at the hotel was called Mr. Louis."

Frank and Joe exchanged knowing glances. Mr. Louis probably was the "L" mentioned in the note Chet had found attached to the downed carrier pigeon.

"How did you expect to get paid for the job, if you didn't know the name of the man who hired you?" Frank asked Ragu.

"He promised to pay me with a ruby ring. It was left in a secret place," Ragu replied. "The only time I wore it was when I came to your house to take the falcon. After that, I was afraid and sold the ring. You know about that."

Frank confirmed this, then Joe asked, "Who hired you to steal our falcon?"

"I don't know that, either," Ragu replied. "I got a phone call at my rooming house. An unfamiliar voice said if I could steal the falcon, I would receive another ruby in payment."

"What part do the pigeons play in this racket?" Frank asked the prisoner.

"They carry messages, but I don't know where they go. And I don't know what the notes say."

Chief Collig turned to Mr. Delhi and asked him if he had any further questions. He had none.

Frank spoke up. "Ragu, tell us about Captain

Flont and his activities. He's more than a fishing boat captain, isn't he?"

Ragu bit his lip. He looked at Mr. Delhi, then settled back on his cot.

"I don't know much about Captain Flont," he said. "I've only worked for him a short time."

No amount of persuasion could elicit any further information from the first mate. It was evident, as Kane had learned, that the crew of the *Daisy K* was afraid of their captain.

"I guess we've found out all we can tonight," said Chief Collig when the visitors left the cell.

On the way back to the Hardy home, Mr. Delhi was silent, but just before they turned into the driveway, he asked, "How will you boys proceed now? When Captain Flont hears of Ragu's arrest he may make trouble."

"We'll have to take that chance," Joe replied. Then he snapped his fingers. "Frank, how about you and I disguising ourselves and joining a fishing party on the *Daisy K* for a day?"

"To do some detecting?"

"Right."

Joe decided to take the falcon indoors for the night. Ragu's arrest might mean trouble, as Mr. Delhi had said. At any rate, the smugglers would be doubly determined to get the hawk.

Mr. Delhi followed the boys through the kitchen door and into the living room where Mrs. Hardy and Aunt Gertrude were reading.

While Joe took the hawk to the boys' room, Frank introduced their visitor to the women. Mrs. Hardy said, "Mr. Delhi, it's much too late for you to start back for Washington. We should like to have you spend the night with us."

"I'm grateful for your thoughtfulness," the man declared. "Thank you. I will accept."

By eleven o'clock the boys and their guest found it impossible to keep from yawning, despite the interesting conversation about the differences in customs between India and the United States. Mrs. Hardy suggested that they retire.

"I shall wait for my husband," she said. "He'll be back about midnight."

The boys were pleased to hear that their father was coming and would have liked to talk to him as soon as he arrived. But they were very sleepy, and also they had to rise early for the fishing trip.

They kissed their mother and aunt good night, then escorted their visitor to the guest room. The boys provided him with pajamas, robe, and slippers.

The three said good night and within half an hour Frank and Joe were sound asleep. But some time later Frank awoke with a start. He glanced at the luminous dial of their alarm clock. It was almost two o'clock.

Joe awoke a moment later and called from his bed, "What's the matter? Is it time to get up?"

"No, it's only two o'clock. But do you hear

someone moving around downstairs?" Frank asked.

"No."

"An intruder couldn't be in the house," Frank mused. "Mother and Dad would have set the burglar alarm before going to bed."

Joe got up and tiptoed across to the door. He opened it and listened for several seconds.

"Not a sound," he reported.

"That's good," Frank replied, stretching and relaxing again. "Now let's go back to sleep."

Joe closed the bedroom door, then walked over to the side window and opened it wider. As he did, he saw something move on the lawn.

"*Psst*—Frank! Come here quick!" His brother was at his side in a second.

"What's up?" Frank asked.

"Someone's down at the edge of the lawn," Joe said. "Over by the hedge."

"Let's throw the spotlights on him," Frank suggested.

The Hardy home had a bright spotlight under the eaves on each side of the house—a precaution occasioned by too many prowlers interested in the detectives' work. The lights were controlled from switches in the upper and lower halls.

"Okay," Joe agreed.

Frank dashed from the room to snap on the second-floor switch. Instantly the front lawn was flooded with light. Outlined against the hedge was

"He's going to throw something!"
Frank whispered

a hooded figure with one arm raised above his head. In that position, he froze for a moment, evidently blinded by the glare.

Frank had rejoined his brother at the window. "Looks as if he was going to throw something!" he whispered.

Before Joe could make a reply, the hooded figure hurled a large, round object straight toward them.

Both boys jumped back. The man missed his mark and the object crashed into a side window of the living room directly below them.

Instantly the burglar alarm clanged, then was drowned out in a deafening roar! The spotlights went out and the Hardy home shuddered on its foundation!

Frank and Joe were flung violently to the floor!

CHAPTER XIV

Doubting a Friend

DAZED by the explosion, Joe Hardy picked himself up in the pitch-dark bedroom and groped about.

"Frank, you okay?" he asked.

There was no reply. Fearful, Joe felt around the floor for his brother but could not find him. Bumping into the bureau which had been shifted out of place by the impact of the blast, Joe opened the top drawer and found a flashlight.

Its beam revealed Frank's unconscious form between the beds.

"His head must have hit the bedpost," Joe decided as he knelt beside his brother.

Frank stirred and opened his eyes.

"Our house was bombed," Joe told him. "Are you all right?"

"Y-yes," Frank replied weakly. With Joe's assistance he stood up.

They opened the door to the hall. A wave of acrid smoke rolled toward them. Through it, they could see their father with a flashlight coming from his room. "I just called the fire department," he said.

"Is everybody all right?" Joe called.

"Your mother is. I don't know about the others."

Behind him, they could now see Mrs. Hardy. A moment later Aunt Gertrude's door flew open. She began to sneeze and cough.

A police siren shrilled and minutes later two fire trucks arrived. Mr. Delhi appeared and everyone went downstairs to survey the damage.

There was no sign of a blaze, but part of one wall in the living room gaped open and the room was a shambles. The boys told the fire chief what they had seen and he checked the house thoroughly for safety.

Since there was no blaze, the trucks left, and the fire chief followed after taking down all the details. By now a crowd of neighbors had gathered and all offered their sympathy and the accommodations of their homes.

"Thank you," Mr. Hardy said to each, "but since the damage is so extensive, I think we'd better move to the Bayport Hotel. It looks as though it will be quite a while before our home will be habitable."

When the neighbors had dispersed, Mr. Delhi

addressed the family. "I'm no doubt responsible for what has happened," he began. "Apparently my identity is known to my enemies, regardless of our precautions last evening. I feel I cannot subject you to further damage and wish to relieve you from the case at once. You have already suffered enough in trying to help me and my country."

Mr. Hardy looked first at his sons, then at their guest. "Mr. Delhi," he replied, "we will see this thing through with you. We can't bow out of a case, especially one that's so near a solution!"

"And I don't believe," Joe put in, "that the bomb was thrown into our house because of you, Mr. Delhi. I saw the fellow aim it directly at Frank and me as we were looking out our bedroom window."

Frank suggested that he and Joe stay at the house to guard it from looters while the others took rooms in the hotel.

Mr. Hardy grinned. "You'll be needed for sleuthing elsewhere. I'll put Jeff Kane here."

After everyone had dressed, and the Hardys had packed a few clothes, they gathered outdoors.

Chief Collig was at the scene now, having been summoned from his home. He had ordered searchlights set up and had stationed men around the Hardy house.

The chief reported that the hard ground had yielded no footprints and that his men had found no clue to the person who had thrown the bomb.

However, in the living room they had found parts of the bomb. The remnants had been collected for the police laboratory to examine.

Satisfied that the situation was under control, Mr. Hardy and the others went to the hotel. It was dawn when they were finally settled in their suite.

By that time all desire for sleep had vanished for everyone except Mr. Hardy. The detective said he had worked late the previous two nights and needed a few hours' rest before tackling several important problems. Not the least of these was the attempt on the lives of himself, his family, and their visitor.

After he had gone to bed, his sons talked with Mr. Delhi about the mystery bombing incident. One thing was certain. The hooded man certainly was not Ragu, since he was still in the Bayport jail.

When the hotel coffee shop opened at six o'clock, the three went in to have breakfast. Halfway through the meal, Mr. Delhi excused himself to make a phone call. He returned, much disturbed.

"Forgive me," he began nervously. "I have just learned that I must fly to New York at once. Should you want to reach me, call Mr. Ghapur. He will know of my whereabouts. And please make my apologies to your family."

"Let us drive you to the airport," Frank offered

The Indian said quickly, "Thank you, no. You have been most kind to me. I shall take a taxi. Good-by."

With that, he strode out the door of the coffee shop. The boys followed him to the hotel entrance. As he climbed into a brown-and-white taxi, they waved farewell.

"What do you suppose upset him so?" Joe said as they returned to the coffee shop.

"He sure acted strange," Frank agreed.

When the boys finished eating, Frank suggested that they drive to their house to search for a clue to the person who had thrown the bomb. Perhaps the police had overlooked something.

It was shortly after seven o'clock when they turned into Elm Street. The story of the explosion had spread all over Bayport, and scores of people had gathered outside the police barricades. One of the officers on guard approached the Hardys and said:

"There's a young fellow over there by the barrier who says you boys would want to see him."

Turning, Frank saw Chet waving at them excitedly and urging a police officer to let him through. Chet hurried to the Hardys, his eyes popping as he studied the damage to their home.

"Gosh, fellows, I'm sorry this happened," he

said. "Is everybody all right?" At a nod from Joe, he went on, "How'd Miss Peregrine take it?"

Frank's and Joe's mouths dropped open. In the excitement they had completely forgotten the prize bird!

They dashed up the porch steps two at a time and ran pell-mell up the stairway. There was only a slim chance that the falcon would still be alive. The door to their room stood ajar and one glance inside revealed the bird's perch lying in a corner.

But the falcon was gone!

After the initial shock was over, Joe said, "She couldn't have flown away, Frank. Her leash was fastened to the ring at the base of the perch stand. It would have to be twisted or broken to free her. Someone took her!"

Frank nodded. "With all the police and by-standers around here, someone must have seen who it was. Let's ask them."

By this time Chet had caught up to the boys and was saying, "I asked you about Miss Peregrine and you acted as if you'd been shot." When the Hardys explained, Chet said, "Maybe the house was bombed so those smugglers could get your bird."

"That might have been part of the plan," Frank conceded, but he was convinced there was much more behind it than that.

The three boys headed back downstairs. They checked with Jeff Kane and the policemen guarding the house, but none of them had seen the hawk, nor had any one of them entered the house since the second shift of men had come on duty at seven o'clock.

"Let's ask some of the people in the crowd if they saw anyone carry off the bird," Joe suggested.

The boys separated and began questioning the bystanders. Finally a woman neighbor approached Frank and said:

"I saw your falcon. About six-thirty this morning, when I was walking my dog, a man in a taxi came up and spoke to the policeman on duty at the front door. He went upstairs with him and they came down a few minutes later with the falcon. The man drove off in the taxi with it."

"Which policeman was it?" Frank asked.

"I don't see him around just now, so I guess he's gone off duty."

"Can you tell us the kind of taxicab the man who took the bird came in?" the boy asked.

"It was a brown-and-white one belonging to the Bayport Taxi Company, I think."

Frank thanked the woman for her information and relayed it to Joe and Chet. Then they got into Chet's jalopy and drove to police headquarters.

They traced the officer and learned that he was at his home. Frank reached him by phone. The man said that the stranger had told him the Hardys wanted him to get the falcon, and he knew just which room the bird was in.

"No, he didn't give his name," the policeman said. "He was dark-skinned and seemed to be in an awful hurry."

The Hardys were astonished. Dark-skinned man. Brown-and-white taxi. Taking the falcon during the time they were finishing breakfast. It all seemed to piece together—unfortunately. Could Mr. Delhi have taken the hawk? Had his phone call to New York prompted this? He certainly had been very much disturbed.

As Frank started to ask the policeman for a fuller description of the thief, the connection was broken. He was about to call the officer again when Joe suggested that they get it from the taxi driver, as well as information on his passenger's destination.

The boys headed for the office of the Bayport Taxi Company, a modern outfit with a fleet of radio-equipped taxis. Convinced of the importance of the Hardys' request, the dispatcher willingly contacted his various drivers.

The one they sought appeared at the office about ten minutes later. Frank explained about the missing falcon and their desire to apprehend the thief. The taxi driver's eyebrows went up.

"I remember the guy all right," he said. "I picked him up in front of the Bayport Hotel at six-thirty this morning.

"After the man collected the falcon from a house on Elm Street," the driver went on, "he ordered me to drive him down to a wharf on the waterfront. I was curious about why he wanted to go there at that early hour. The guy said that someone was going to pick him up in a boat."

"Could you give us a description of this man?" Frank asked excitedly.

The taxi driver furrowed his brow for a moment, then replied, "Well, he was young and good-looking and dark-skinned, like one of them Indian rug makers down at Ahmed's place. And he had a scar on his chin. I mean a scar that really stood out—looked lighter than the rest of his skin."

Frank exchanged glances with Joe. They both heaved a sigh of relief. The falcon thief was not Mr. Delhi after all! It must have been the Indian who had bought pigeons from Mr. Newton two years before—the impostor who had used Mr. Delhi's real name of Bhagnav!

The driver noticed the boys' amazed expressions and asked, "Does that description help you?"

"It sure does," Frank said. "Thanks a lot. Now will you drive us to the wharf where you took this passenger? He may still be there."

The three boys climbed into the taxi. Moments later the driver let them out on one of the wharves and promised to wait. They hurried down the length of the dock, but the dark-skinned man was not in sight. No one they questioned on the small boats at the dock had seen anyone carrying a hooded hawk.

"Looks like a dead end," Joe declared in disappointment.

Frank agreed, but Chet tried to cheer them up, saying:

"Listen, fellows, you're due for a real break. Wait and see!"

The Hardys smiled at Chet's words of encouragement and Frank said, "We'd better go to the hotel and brief Dad on this latest development. He ought to be awake by now."

The taxi driver took them back to Chet's jalopy, and Chet in turn drove the Hardys to pick up their car at their home. Then Joe and Frank headed for the hotel.

Mr. and Mrs. Hardy and Aunt Gertrude listened in amazement to the boys' story. When it was finished, their father leaned forward intently in his chair and reached for the telephone.

"I think we have our man," he said as he lifted the phone and waited for the operator. "The light-colored scar on the chin is the giveaway. The description fits an Indian by the name of Nanab. He is Rahmud Ghapur's personal servant!"

CHAPTER XV

A Nautical Clue

TEN minutes later Mr. Hardy placed the phone in its cradle and turned to his sons. "Well, boys, the pieces are beginning to fall into place. Ghapur says that his servant Nanab quit his job very suddenly the day before yesterday and has disappeared."

"Wow!" cried Joe, adding, "Why didn't Mr. Delhi identify him from our description. He must have seen Nanab at Ghapur's home?"

"Nanab apparently kept out of his sight on purpose," Mr. Hardy replied. "He may have feared he might be recognized. The only relative in India that Nanab wrote to while he was in Washington was a brother whose name is Bangalore. So far as Ghapur knows, Bangalore is still in India."

Frank said excitedly, "No, he isn't, Dad. You were away when we learned that Bangalore was the name of an Indian who jumped ship on the

Continental while the vessel was docked in New York. That happened two years ago."

As he finished speaking, Radley came in, holding an envelope. He said he had been to the house and was amazed to learn of the bombing and was relieved to see that the Hardys were safe. He handed over the envelope, saying:

"I got this in the mail. When I opened it, I knew you boys would want to see it." He held up a photograph. "It's a picture of that fellow Bangalore. The steamship line sent it."

"Bangalore!" Mr. Hardy exclaimed. "He's Nanab's brother all right. Looks just like him, except that he has no chin scar. Good work, fellows. It certainly seems as if Bangalore is one of the ringleaders in this smuggling and kidnapping business. Nanab has probably been working with him part of the time and is now spending full time on the rackets."

"Dad, do you think he could have been the one who intercepted Mr. Ghapur's letter to us?" Joe asked.

"No doubt of it. Unfortunately, Ghapur trusted Nanab implicitly and always confided in him. Nanab destroyed the letter, but why do you suppose he let the falcon get through to you?"

"That does seem strange," Frank agreed. "Anyway, we know he learned all the plans and developments in the case by eavesdropping on Ghapur and Mr. Delhi."

"There's one bright side to this whole thing," said his father. "You boys must be much nearer a solution than you think, or I doubt that Nanab would have left his job at Ghapur's. He probably knew the net was closing around him."

Frank and Joe, certain that part of the solution was to be found on the *Daisy K*, determined to carry through with their fishing plan. Since it was too late for the trip scheduled for that day, Frank phoned the booking office for Bayport's charter boats to find out if the *Daisy K* was going out the following morning. He was told there would be a trip.

Mr. Hardy said he would make the necessary arrangements for repairs to their home, then he must return to Washington on urgent business.

The phone rang and Joe answered. The caller was Chet, who said, "How about you fellows coming out here to live until your house is repaired? The folks say it's fine with them."

"Sounds good, Chet. Wait till I ask Dad and Mother."

The family agreed that the boys would find it far more enjoyable staying with Chet than living in the hotel, so Joe promptly accepted. Then, at their parents' request, Frank and Joe worked nearly all day at the bombed house storing away pictures, lamps, and other small furnishings, and moving clothes to the hotel. It was late afternoon when they arrived at the Morton farm.

"Before it gets dark today," Frank proposed, "let's go over to the deserted hunting lodge and see if Radley has anything new to report."

After the Hardys had deposited their luggage in the Mortons' guest room, the three boys set off for the lodge. Radley said there was no evidence that anyone had returned to the lodge and felt further watch of it was useless. He remarked that he would like to tackle the mystery from another angle.

"I've had a lot of time to think out here," he said, "and I came up with an idea. Maybe these smugglers don't send their pigeons from a boat at all. They may be working from an island."

"An island! Could be!" Joe replied enthusiastically. "When we get back to Chet's, let's take a look at a map to see what's northeast of here."

"And," said Radley, "why not let me take a plane and see if I can spot something out there."

"Okay," Frank agreed. "Joe and I are planning a fishing trip on the *Daisy K* early tomorrow morning. Among the three of us we may uncover something either on the sea or from the air."

Radley and the boys walked back to the Morton home where they pored over a map.

"Hm!" said Radley. "Islands galore northeast of here. The closest ones are Shoals, Pine Haven, and Venus, but that doesn't mean they're the ones. The smugglers may be taking no chances and using an island quite a distance away. I'll look over as many as I can from the plane, though."

That evening, after Radley had left, Frank and Joe got their fishing gear ready and tried out their disguises. Their father, an expert in that field, had taught his sons many of the techniques, and they kept all the prerequisites on hand. Hair dye, cheek pads and sideburns changed the countenance of the boys. Dyed eyebrows and a small beard for Frank completed their outfits.

Iola and Chet laughed when they saw Frank and Joe. "You look rather cute as a redhead," Iola told Joe, who had tinted his hair a reddish brown.

Before dawn the next morning, the Hardys set out through a drizzle for the wharf where the *Daisy K* was tied up. Four other sports fishermen already were there, waiting to go aboard. Frank and Joe kept a wary eye on Captain Flont, who did not give any indication that he recognized them. In fact, he paid little attention to his passengers.

The day's fishing went along with reasonable success. All of the *Daisy K*'s passengers managed to net a fair-sized catch of tuna and mackerel. Under various pretexts during the trip, both Frank and Joe wandered around the ship, but the falcon was not aboard. The boys had also made a point of trying to pick up conversations between the captain, his crew of two, and any passengers that might be in league with him, but learned nothing.

In the late afternoon, when the *Daisy K* started back for Bayport, Frank and Joe were seated inside the deckhouse as close as they dared to Captain Flont, who was at the wheel.

Suddenly, above the throbbing of the motors, they heard him say to one of his crew, "It beats me where Ragu went."

"I'm afraid he's in trouble," the man replied.

"It's going to be hard to take care of things at windward without him," the captain said, then shifted the conversation to another subject.

The Hardys got up and walked out to the stern of the boat. When they were alone, Frank whispered, "Did you have the same thought I did? That it was strange for a nautical man to say '*at* windward'?"

"I sure did," Joe replied. "If he had meant a direction, the captain would have said 'to windward.' "

"Right. Windward must be a place!"

The *Daisy K* reached port just before dinner. As Frank and Joe walked along the waterfront with their day's catch of fish, they questioned sailors from other boats about Windward. No one had heard of it. Finally they headed for the hotel, deciding to have supper with the family before going to Chet's.

The young detectives, still in their disguises, turned their mackerel over to a startled bellhop and asked him to deliver them to the hotel chef.

Then, learning from the desk clerk that Radley was waiting for them, they went at once to their room. The detective grinned at their disguise. While they were removing the make-up, he said:

"I flew all over the coast for about five hours, but I couldn't spot any activity that would indicate smuggling operations. I did see several deserted sections along the shores of some of the islands that would make good hideaways. Guess we'll have to investigate all of them."

"Ever hear of a place called Windward?" Frank inquired.

"No," Radley replied. "What about it?"

Frank repeated the conversation that he and Joe had overheard on the *Daisy K.* Radley nodded thoughtfully, then remarked:

"Let's go down to the Skippers Club. I know some of the seafaring men who stay there. Maybe one of them will be able to help us out."

After dinner with Mrs. Hardy and Aunt Gertrude, the three went to the saltbox building near the waterfront, where many of the old-timers played cribbage, chess, and billiards in between spinning sea yarns about the good old days. Sam Radley was hailed by several of the captains. He quizzed some of them about Windward. The name meant nothing to the first half dozen he spoke to, but finally a grizzled man of the sea looked up from a game of solitaire.

"Sure, I know the place. Windward was our

old-timers' name for the windside o' Venus Island," he said. "The lee side's green an' right pretty. Folks live there. But Windward's rocky an' barren. Broken up by stretches o' pine woods here an' there."

Radley thanked the old salt and the three left the club. Outside, Frank remarked, "That sounds like an ideal spot for smuggling operations!"

"Let's check on it right away," Joe proposed. "Maybe we can round up some of the fellows to help us."

"As a matter of fact," said Frank, "Biff Hooper and Tony Prito were planning to go out to Chet's tonight. Let's put all three of them to work on the case."

Radley was eager to go along. They stopped at a drugstore with a couple of phone booths. Joe called Chet to explain their plan to take the *Sleuth* out to Venus Island for a reconnoitering expedition.

"Sounds like a dangerous job," said Chet, "but I'll come and bring Tony and Biff. I expect them here any minute."

"Meet us at our boathouse," Joe said. "And make it as soon as you can."

Frank, meanwhile, had called the hotel from the other booth to apprise his mother of their plans. Next he put in a call to Chief Collig to tell him of their new lead and to ask if Ragu had had any visitors.

"No, and it doesn't look as if he's going to have any, either," Collig replied. "He refuses to see anyone, even an attorney! And he's made no attempt to raise the bail money. Frank, that fellow is plenty scared of somebody!"

"My guess," Frank said, "is that it's Captain Flont!" He said good-by and hung up. Then he drove to the boathouse with Radley and Joe. A quick look around showed that repairs were well under way and that the *Sleuth* could be returned to its berth before long.

Presently Chet's jalopy rattled up the street and pulled to a stop. Lanky, good-natured Biff Hooper swung his long legs over the side, and Tony Prito followed. Chet squeezed himself out of the driver's seat and joined the group. They all walked to the *Sleuth* and went aboard. Frank took them across Barmet Bay, out through the inlet, and into the swells of the ocean beyond. It was just past midnight when Frank outlined the Hardys' plans.

"When we get to Windward, we'll cruise around and find out what we can," he said. "If we don't learn anything, then Joe and Radley and I will go ashore to investigate."

Tony, who owned a boat of his own, would be left in charge of the *Sleuth*.

Two hours later the forbidding rocky slopes of Windward were etched in black against the moonlit sky. The motor of the *Sleuth* was throttled down and a search of the waters began. They found no boats anchored and none were visible in any of the many inlets among the rocks.

At three-fifteen Radley and the Hardys decided to go ashore. They donned their swim trunks and slid over the side without a sound.

Treading water beside the boat, Frank said in a low voice to the boys in the *Sleuth*, "You fellows cruise back and forth, keeping your eyes open for anything that might be stirring. We'll swim out again just at daybreak and meet you."

Chet, Tony, and Biff wished them luck, then started off. They cruised around for some time without seeing another boat or sighting anything suspicious. Finally, as the first streak of dawn appeared in the east, Tony moved the *Sleuth* to the spot where they had left the swimmers.

After what seemed like a long wait, Tony said, "Fellows, I'm worried. Frank, Joe, and Radley are overdue."

The three in the boat could not see anyone along the shore or in the water that lay between the *Sleuth* and the rocky beach. Tony moved the boat a little closer and got out the binoculars. There was not a sign of anyone on the rocks.

"I'll—I'll bet the smugglers got them!" Chet said nervously. "What'll we do now?"

"Give them fifteen minutes," Tony advised, "and then storm that island!"

CHAPTER XVI

Forbidding Island

FRANK, Joe, and Radley had swum easily to the narrow, rocky beach on the windward side of Venus Island. The water was chilly, but their brisk strokes had kept them from feeling the cold.

A jagged cliff that rose abruptly about twenty feet back from the shore was clearly outlined in the moonlight. Before emerging from the surf, the swimmers had made sure that no guard was on duty on the beach. They gazed around the desolate shore but could see no evidence of anyone having been there recently.

Frank mused, "Footprints or signs of beaching a boat could have been washed out by the waves."

They climbed a trail that wound up the face of the cliff and turned their attention to a woods of windswept pines, which came to within a hundred feet of the cliff's edge. The three sleuths peered ahead.

Frank spied a light among the trees. "I wonder

if that light is coming from a house. I thought this area of the island was uninhabited."

"Let's find out," Joe urged.

They found a path among the trees and followed it until Joe held up his hand in warning.

"I think I hear voices!"

He and the others paused to listen. Not far from them several men were talking, part of the time in English, part in a foreign tongue the trio had come to recognize as a dialect of India.

The Hardys and Radley crouched behind a clump of bushes, trying to fathom the conversation. The voices carried clearly on the night air, and the listeners were provoked at not being able to translate the foreign words. Presently the watchers were electrified upon hearing:

"Cap's late. I hope he didn't run into trouble. A motorboat was cruising around here a while ago. Better go take a look."

There was no verbal response to the command, but a blond man began to walk toward the watchers' hiding place. After he had gone a short distance, they followed silently, hoping the *Sleuth* was now far enough from the island not to be noticed.

"If that fellow has a boat hidden nearby and decides to set out for the *Sleuth*," Joe whispered tensely, "we'll jump him!"

"Right!" Frank replied.

The man paused briefly at the edge of the cliff,

then gingerly made his way down the trail to the beach. Radley and the Hardys crept to the brink and peered below. They did not see the *Sleuth*, but a surprise awaited them. A large motor dory, its engine off, was being propelled by oars toward the beach. As they watched, it glided to a stop just beyond the rocky shore. The watchers could see two men in the dory, but the figures were not close enough to be identified.

"Say, Frank," Joe whispered, "that sure looks like the same dory that met the *Daisy K* the night of the moonlight ride."

The blond man on the stony shore gave a low whistle. Almost instantly Radley and the boys became aware of tramping feet and a few moments later a dozen dark-skinned men, carrying trousers and shoes, came down the trail, passing just a few feet from the three in hiding. They were followed by a light-haired man. When they reached the beach, he pointed to the dory and immediately the men splashed through the waves toward it.

"Smuggled Indians!" Joe said in a hoarse whisper. "Let's try to stop them!"

Radley gripped Joe's arm. "That would only mean our capture. They outnumber us almost six to one!"

Joe calmed down as the aliens climbed aboard and the oars dipped into the surf. The dory was some distance from shore before its engine was started.

As the two islanders came up the path and moved off among the trees, Frank whispered to Joe:

"Those men obviously are guards here," he said. "Do you suppose they're the two we watched being transferred from the *Daisy K* to the dory?"

"Come on!" Joe urged. "Let's collar them!"

He sprang into action. Without a backward glance to see if the others were following, he set off on a run among the trees after the blond men.

Frank and Radley tried to stop Joe. They hurried after him, but within a few seconds, they heard sounds of a struggle.

"Joe ran into trouble," Frank said in a tense whisper.

Minutes later they spotted the two guards prodding Joe toward a group of small buildings set deep in a grove and almost hidden from view. One of the men kicked open the door of the nearest building and Joe was thrust into a lighted room.

"We've got to free him!" Frank said. "This gang will stop at nothing!"

Radley restrained him. "Hold it, Frank," he said sternly. "Look what happened to Joe. The thing to do is to outwit these men."

"You're right," Frank replied. "Tell you what," he said, noticing that the sky was lightening. "Tony, Chet, and Biff will be waiting offshore. Suppose you swim out to the *Sleuth* and try to follow the dory with the aliens in it. See where it goes. Then bring help back here. In the meantime, I'll try to think up a way to free Joe and maybe pick up more evidence."

His companion nodded and left at once. Frank waited until he heard the familiar roar of the *Sleuth*'s engine as it took off at high speed, before he started his own work. Moving swiftly and cautiously, he edged in close to the building where Joe was imprisoned.

Through a closed window he saw that his brother had been bound to a chair. A coil of rope and a knife lay on a nearby table.

As he watched helplessly, the two middle-aged guards began cuffing Joe's face. Quickly Frank moved to another window which was open. He heard one of the guards say:

"This kid just won't talk. Put the gag back in."

"I don't buy his story," the other man said as he replaced the gag, "that he came to Windward to swim all by himself in the middle of the night. He's a spy. We ought to check the area to see if there are any pals of his lurking around."

Frank ducked around the corner just in time. For, an instant later, the door of the cabin burst open and the two men rushed out. Frank, desperately realizing he must conceal himself, dodged behind a tree.

One of the guards announced he would circle the cabin. Frank held his breath, as the man passed without noticing him. The other zig-zagged through the woods between the house and the beach, looking for trespassers, but shortly returned to report there was no evidence of other intruders.

The two men re-entered the house. Frank returned to the open window. There was no possible way he could move in on Joe's captors without being seen.

A few minutes later one of the guards said, "Keep an eye on our prisoner while I go to eat breakfast. I'll spell you later, after I've talked to Cap. I've got a hunch about this kid!"

Frank wondered what he meant by the last statement, then smiled triumphantly. This was his chance to free Joe!

He ducked into hiding again as the guard came out, closed the door behind him, and walked toward one of the other buildings. Frank waited until the man had entered the cabin, which stood about a hundred yards away, then quietly moved to the door of Joe's prison and slowly turned the knob. The door was unlocked!

Picking up a piece of shale from the path, Frank threw it at a windowpane. When the piece of rock crashed through, Joe's guard whirled away from the boy's side and dashed to the window. At the same time, Frank flattened himself against the door, his hand on the knob. As the guard gingerly leaned out the shattered window, Frank eased open the door and entered the room, his bare feet making no sound.

With lightning speed Frank whipped the gag from Joe's mouth with one hand, and with the other grabbed a knife from the table and slashed at the rope which bound Joe's hands.

This was barely accomplished when the man at the window pulled his head in. Before he could turn, Frank gripped him around the throat, stuffed the gag in his mouth, and caught one of his arms in a judo hold. Then he threw him to the floor. Joe quickly bound the guard with the rope that had seconds before secured him.

The prisoner glared at the Hardys as they consulted in low tones. "I sure messed this deal up," Joe remarked ruefully. "Thanks for turning the tables."

Frank grinned understandingly. "I'll keep a lookout in this room while you investigate the rest of the cabin," he said. "If that other guard heard the glass breaking, he'll come to see what happened."

Joe picked up a flashlight from the table in order to explore the dark rooms beyond. Frank posted himself at the door. In a few seconds Joe was back at his brother's side.

"There are two more rooms in this building," Joe reported. "One's locked and—what do you know?—in the other there are five carrier pigeons in cages!"

Frank was excited at this news. "That clinches it. We've come to the right place. Let's go see if we can find out if Cap is who I think he is."

The boys checked the bonds on their prisoner, then rolled him under one of the bunks which lined two walls, and left the cabin. As they approached the building which the other guard had entered, Frank pointed out a high radio aerial that rose from the roof. "They have a powerful set," he said.

Both boys peered cautiously in a window, and noted that it must be the building where the guards and the aliens ate their meals. At one end was an old-fashioned cooking stove. Two long dining tables, capable of seating a large number of people, stood at the other side of the big room.

Seated at a smaller table which stood against the far wall was the guard. In front of him was a short-wave sending-and-receiving radio. Over it, he was sending the startling message:

"We've captured a spy. From your description, I think he's one of those Hardy boys!"

Frank and Joe gulped. The news was out! But no more must be sent!

Joe sprang through the doorway and threw himself at the man, knocking him away from the instrument and clipping him soundly on the jaw. The man sprawled on the floor, unconscious.

With the mike switch released, the transmitter was cut off. Frank, who had followed his brother into the room, instantly turned on the receiver. The cold, hard voice of Captain Flont was saying:

"We're being followed! I'm going to open fire!"

Terror in their eyes, Frank's and Joe's hearts sank.

"The *Sleuth!*" both boys thought. "It must be the *Sleuth* that Captain Flont has spotted!"

CHAPTER XVII

An Escaped Prisoner

A FEELING of hopelessness swept over Frank and Joe. There was no way to warn their friends that Captain Flont intended to fire on them!

Frank paced up and down the cabin, clenching his fists. Then, suddenly, he thought of a way in which Captain Flont might be tricked.

Grabbing a paper napkin from one of the dining tables, Frank wrapped it around the mouthpiece of the short-wave microphone. Perhaps the napkin would muffle his voice enough to prevent its being recognized. He pressed the mike switch.

"Flont! Don't shoot! Orders from the boss!"

Frank clicked on the receiver but there was no answer. He kept repeating "Come in, Flont." Still no reply. As Joe looked on tensely, Frank continued this call intermittently for ten minutes. Finally, receiving no response from the captain, he gave up.

"Maybe Flont had turned off his set before I started sending the order," Frank said, worried. "Or he may have recognized my voice."

"You tried the only thing possible," Joe said. "Besides, even though there wasn't any answer, Flont might have heard it and been fooled. All we can do is hope."

Joe suggested that he hurry across to the other side of the island and contact the local police. "In the meantime, you stand by the radio, just in case Flont should call in again."

"Okay," Frank agreed. "But let's tie this fellow up first."

They bound the captive's ankles and arms, and put a gag in his mouth. Joe found a pair of shoes and a sweater, put them on, and started off.

He located a rocky trail and followed it a couple of miles, until he came out of the woods. Finally, nearly an hour after leaving the smugglers' cabin, Joe spotted a farmhouse and dashed up to it.

Fortunately the residents were awake. They listened with some skepticism to the boy's story. But they permitted Joe to use their phone and offered to drive him to the chief of police in Venus Village.

But Joe could not get through to either Chief Collig or his mother at the Bayport Hotel, due to the inadequate service between the island and Bayport. After several attempts, however, he finally contacted the Coast Guard. The young detective was told that men would be sent out at once to apprehend Captain Flont and learn what had happened to the *Sleuth*.

On the drive to town the farmer remarked, "This is the first time I remember anything happening around here which needed the police. Chief Barton's appointment was kind of an honorary one."

When the farmer stopped at the police chief's home in Venus Village, Joe thanked him for the lift, then rang the bell.

Chief Barton was a man past middle age, with a paunch and a good-natured smile.

"Well, what brings you around here so early in the morning, stranger?" the man asked.

"I'm Joe Hardy from Bayport. My brother and I have located the hideout of a ring of smugglers here on Venus Island. We've got two of them tied up. We'd like you to come and make the arrests."

"Smugglers on Venus Island!" The chief roared with laughter. "Who you trying to kid, son?"

"It's true," Joe insisted, trying not to show annoyance. "The Coast Guard and the immigration authorities have been trying to track them down for months. The State Department's interested, too!"

"How does the State Department figure in this?" the officer asked curiously.

"These smugglers are also kidnappers," Joe

said. "They're holding a young Indian captive."

The man finally seemed to realize the seriousness of the situation and said, "Well, no one can say that Chief Barton doesn't tend to business. I'll phone my deputy and we'll be right with you. Just sit down in the parlor."

It seemed an eternity to Joe while Barton made the contact with his deputy and dressed. But at last the chief brought in a tall, lanky man whom he introduced as Al Richards. The deputy studied Joe for a moment, then commented:

"So you're one of the Hardy boys, eh? I've heard about you fellows down around Bayport. What's this wild-goose chase we're going on?"

"Smugglers!" Joe said tersely. "And let's get going before it's too late."

The three drove part way back to the smugglers' hideout in a jeep. They stopped about a mile from the cabins, and Joe led the men the rest of the way on foot. A fork in the path brought them to the first cabin.

Frank, who had found shoes and a shirt, heard them coming and went to meet the group. He said he certainly was glad to see the police, and reported that no radio messages had been received.

"One of the smugglers is in here," he told the men as they paused at the cabin door.

"Well," drawled Deputy Richards, "we're ready for him. Let's see what a smuggler looks like."

They opened the door and Joe walked across to the bunk. He knelt down to pull out the trussed-up man.

The prisoner was not there!

"He's gone!" Joe cried.

"Gone!" echoed Frank. "But how?"

Deputy Richards remarked laconically, "Told you this would be a wild-goose chase!"

The chief shook his head slowly and shrugged, eying the Hardys dubiously. Frank and Joe were staring at each other, blaming themselves for the prisoner's getaway. Apparently they had not tied him securely enough.

But perhaps he had not had time to go far, the boys thought. In fact, he might still be in the building! They dashed into the adjoining room. The escaped man was not there and only three of the pigeons were left in the cages.

Frank tried the door to the next room—the one Joe had reported locked. It was unlocked now.

As the door swung open a wholly unexpected scene met their eyes. Joe cried out, "Here he is!" and Frank yelled, "Stop!"

The police chief and his deputy rushed in. At an open window stood the man who had been the Hardys' prisoner. He was releasing two carrier pigeons.

Joe, noticing there were capsules on the birds' legs, leaped forward to stop their flight. But he was too late!

"Here he is!" Joe cried out

"Where are those messages going?" he demanded, but the man made no reply.

Frank spotted a large perch in a corner. On it rested a hooded hawk. Certain that the falcon was their own, he picked up a heavy leather gauntlet from a window sill. Quickly donning the glove, Frank took the bird on his wrist. As he removed the hood, Frank spoke softly to her. The hawk recognized him instantly and uttered a joyful *keer, keer*.

Frank turned to the police officers and said, "Here is support for our story. This is a prize hunting hawk, and it was stolen from our home in Bayport."

"Arrest this man!" Joe said. "He's in cahoots with the thief and he's one of the smugglers."

Chief Barton made no move to take the man into custody. Instead, he stared at the smuggler. "Why, John Cullen, what's going on?" he asked.

Frank was puzzled by the chief's friendliness, but he did not take time to ask questions. He was afraid that the pigeons might be carrying messages which would alert the men holding Tava Nayyar. If so, harm might come to the youth. Frank hurried outside with the falcon and unhooded her.

Looking up, he saw that the carrier pigeons were circling above the cabin, picking up their directional beam preparatory to making a beeline flight to their destination.

Frank turned the falcon loose. To his dismay, she responded sluggishly. Her reactions were considerably slowed down as a result of being imprisoned for so long. There was nothing the impatient young detective could do to hasten matters. He must wait until she regained her keenness.

At that moment Chief Barton and Deputy Richards came out of the cabin with John Cullen and Joe. In an angry tone the chief of police said to the Hardys:

"If your whole story's as phony as this part of it, I'm afraid we can't help you."

"What do you mean?" Joe demanded.

"This so-called smuggler, Mr. Cullen, is one of the leading citizens on the island, though he has only lived here a couple of years. He's a pigeon fancier and has been racing birds for a year or more. His cote's on the mainland."

The Hardys were not impressed. Turning to Cullen, Joe asked suspiciously:

"How do you account for our stolen falcon being in your cabin?"

"My assistant got furiously angry about the whole deal, I'm afraid," the man replied suavely.

"What deal?" Joe probed.

"He knew that a number of my best pigeons had been killed by a hunting hawk. Someone told him that your falcon was responsible."

Frank's and Joe's minds were racing. Suddenly

a thought came to them. *Nanab!* He had doubtless brought the falcon to the island!

"Go on!" Frank said icily to Cullen.

"My assistant brought the bird here, so that I could use it as evidence in my damage suit against you," the man concluded triumphantly.

It was obvious that both Chief Barton and Deputy Richards believed the story and were about to reproach the boys when Joe challenged Cullen with:

"That sounds smooth enough. Now try to explain why the other man we captured was talking by short-wave to a boat with smuggled aliens on it."

"You're crazy," Cullen retorted. "Chief Barton, these boys are the ones who ought to be arrested!"

All this time Frank had not taken his eyes off the falcon. She had finally aroused from her lethargy and was now winging after the two pigeons. The hawk was still some distance from the birds, who were lining out for the mainland. Completely confident of the falcon's skill, Frank remarked:

"Chief Barton, maybe our hunting hawk will prove to you that Mr. Cullen is not merely racing pigeons. *She* may prove he is aiding smugglers and kidnappers!"

All eyes turned toward the three birds in the morning sky.

CHAPTER XVIII

The Falcon's Victory

THE falcon was only a tiny speck in the sky. The pigeons were out over the water but well below the climbing hawk. Frank turned to Joe and said:

"I guess this is what those old-time falconers called a 'ringing flight.' I'm going to the beach to watch it." The others followed him.

At the height of her pitch, the falcon plunged toward the pigeons in a long, angling stoop. Faster and faster she dropped—until the onlookers saw only a blur of moving wings. At a speed approaching a hundred and eighty miles an hour the hawk struck one of the pigeons. It plummeted into the water.

The peregrine mounted from her stoop and gave chase to the remaining pigeon.

Frank shouted, "Joe, take this and watch Cullen!" He thrust the hawk's hood into Joe's hand,

153

kicked off his shoes, and ran into the surf. He set off at a strong, fast crawl toward the floating pigeon and soon reached it.

As Frank swam toward the beach with it, he glanced up. The second pigeon had reversed its course and was heading toward the brushy cover of the island. With awe and admiration he and Joe watched their falcon overtake her prey in a tail chase and bind to it in mid-air. In a long glide Miss Peregrine came to rest with her quarry in her talons.

"Good girl!" Joe cried. He ran forward and picked up the pigeon.

At that moment Frank came out of the surf and joined Joe. John Cullen cried angrily, "Leave those birds alone! They're my property!" With a vicious lunge he grabbed for both of them.

To the boys' dismay Chief Barton said, "I guess he's right, fellows. Let him have the birds."

Frank and Joe were nonplussed. "I'll give them to you, Chief, but not to this man," Frank said firmly.

Frank quickly flipped the capsule off the leg of the pigeon he was holding, while Joe removed the one on the other bird. Cullen tried to snatch the capsules, screaming in a hysterical voice that this was thievery and against the law. He demanded that the policemen do something.

But the chief and his deputy were stunned by

the swift-moving events. Before the men could collect their wits, the Hardys had twisted open the tops of the capsules.

Two rubies dropped into Frank's hand!

Joe's capsule contained a tightly folded note, which he opened and read aloud:

" 'Twelve a's gone. Spies here. We're leaving island. Advise you move at once.' "

Chief Barton stared in amazement. Turning to Cullen, he demanded, "What does this mean?"

But Cullen was already fleeing pell-mell over the rocks.

"I guess that proves he's guilty!" Joe exclaimed. "Twelve a's must mean those aliens who left here in the dory!"

Stuffing the note into his pocket, he dashed after Cullen, with the police at his heels. The chase was soon over. As the fugitive attempted to get away in a motorboat hidden in a cove, he was caught and marched back.

"I guess you're not innocent after all," said Chief Barton. "But you sure had me fooled."

Cullen looked with hatred at the Hardys. "You idiots!" he snarled. "I'll get you for this!"

Frank suggested to the officers that they pick up the other smuggler at once. Silently he and Joe hoped the man had not been able to loosen his bonds and send a radio message!

Joe hooded the falcon and led the way to the

second cabin. They found the man on the floor, still bound and gagged. Chief Barton stared at him, then exclaimed in amazement:

"Arthur Daly! You're mixed up with the smugglers, too!" He turned to the boys and remarked, "Mr. Daly owns one of the most successful lobster businesses in this area."

The Hardys did not comment, but Frank said, "I suggest you handcuff these men."

At a gesture from Barton, Deputy Richards took care of this detail. Then the chief advised his prisoners of their rights. Both sullenly declared they did not want a lawyer.

"How about telling us the truth now about this whole thing!" Barton said. "We'll find it out anyhow."

The men refused to talk, but the Hardys explained what they knew of the illicit entries of the Indians, the kidnapping of Tava Nayyar, and the ransom demanded in rubies.

"The pigeons carried the stones and notes from here to their home cote," said Joe. "And that's the next place we'll have to locate."

Barton shook his head in amazement. "And we had no idea that something like this was going on at Windward!"

His deputy nodded. "You two have done quite a job!"

"We'll take these men to jail and notify the Federal authorities," Barton said. He suggested that they all proceed to town at once. Carrying the falcon and the three remaining pigeons, the group headed for the jeep.

Barton promised to station men at Windward to arrest any smugglers who might show up.

Back at Venus Village, the once respected islanders were put in cells, then Barton dispatched special deputies to the Windward area. Next, he talked by phone to the immigration authorities. Ten minutes later, a broad smile on his face, he leaned back in his chair and said:

"Things are moving along fine. Federal men will be out soon to take over."

"Good," said Joe. "And now may I phone the Coast Guard? I want to find out what happened to the friends who came out here with us."

"Go ahead," the chief replied.

At the first words of Lieutenant Commander Wilson, who answered, Joe looked relieved. He put his hand over the mouthpiece and said to Frank, "They caught Flont and his two crewmen as well as those twelve smuggled aliens! They're at the Coast Guard station now."

As Joe listened intently to the lieutenant commander he sobered. When he hung up the phone, he reported that there was no news of their friends. Flont would not say whether he had fired on them before his capture. A Coast Guard helicopter was out now searching for the *Sleuth*.

The Hardys were worried. Frank asked, "Chief,

could someone take us back to the mainland right away?"

"Sure thing," Barton agreed. "I'll run you to Bayport myself in my own motorboat. And, say, will you fellows take these pigeons? I don't know what to do with 'em and you might find the birds useful."

"Okay. We will," said Frank.

Barton kept his boat in good shape, and a little over an hour later, the chief, Frank and Joe, the hooded hawk and the three pigeons were speeding across Barmet Bay toward Bayport.

Joe, who had been scanning the water through binoculars, suddenly called, "There's the *Sleuth* now, Frank!"

About a quarter of a mile ahead was the Hardys' boat. Barton sounded his siren and minutes later he drew alongside the *Sleuth*.

"You all right?" Frank and Joe asked.

Upon being assured that Chet, Tony, Biff, and Radley were unharmed, Frank introduced the police chief.

Chet, his eyes bulging, exclaimed, "You got the falcon back! And are those the smugglers' pigeons?"

"They sure are," Barton replied. "And we got the ringleaders behind bars, too!"

Frank and Joe let the last statement go unchallenged, even though they knew the hardest part of the case—catching the real ringleaders—

still faced them. They told their friends that Captain Flont had been captured, then asked what had happened to the group in the *Sleuth*.

"We g-got fired on," Chet answered promptly. "The captain missed, thank goodness, and he didn't try again. I don't know why."

"Because Frank short-waved him not to," Joe said, and explained about the radio message. "Then what happened?"

Tony, Chet, and Biff tried to tell the story at the same time. Quickly Radley summarized the situation.

"We picked up the trail of the *Daisy K* shortly after I swam back to the *Sleuth*. Flont had already taken aboard the smuggled Indians from the dory. He had a long-range rifle and we were his target! I think Flont fired the first shot to scare us, because I don't see how he could have missed!

"Before he could follow it up with another, Frank's message must have reached him. Anyway, he stopped firing and started off, full speed ahead. When we followed, he kept the rifle trained on us. We finally gave up the chase, deciding to make a wide sweep around him, then race to shore and send the Coast Guard out for the *Daisy K*."

Radley went on to say that as they headed for a cove, the *Sleuth* ran out of gas. "And to make matters worse," he continued with a wry smile, "the emergency fuel can was empty."

The operative said that another boat had finally come by. As it was transferring fuel, the Coast Guard helicopter flew over, hovered above them, and dropped a note instructing them to proceed to Bayport.

When Frank and Joe finished comparing notes with their friends on the night's adventures, the Hardys climbed into their own boat, taking the birds with them. The police chief promised to keep them informed of developments on the island.

As soon as they reached Bayport, Radley and the Hardys headed for the Coast Guard station. There Lieutenant Commander Wilson was questioning the prisoners, who had been properly advised of their rights. He had been in touch with Washington, and was impressed with the importance of the capture. He looked up as Frank, Joe, and Radley entered and motioned them toward empty chairs alongside his desk.

Captain Flont glared at the Hardys as he was asked to repeat his statement.

"I've told you a dozen times I'm innocent," he declared. "I didn't know those Indians were aliens. Someone radioed to me that a party of picnickers had been stranded on Venus Island. They offered to pay me my usual fishing fee to bring them back to Bayport."

Radley asked, "Why did you fire on the *Sleuth?*"

Flont was ready with an answer. "You were

following us, and it made my passengers nervous. I just fired in the air to scare you."

Frank walked over to the group of aliens and asked if any of them spoke English. One young man came forward.

Before he could say anything, Flont's face turned purple with anger and he shouted, "You men keep your mouths shut!"

The Indian looked frightened, turned, and talked with the other aliens for some time. Then he faced Frank with determination. "We pay these men lot of money for bring us to this country. Now bad trouble. We want to go home!"

Frank said to the lieutenant commander, "I guess you've got your evidence."

"One more question," said Joe, looking at the young Indian. "While you were with these men who were trying to smuggle you in, did you ever hear anything about the kidnapping of Tava Nayyar?"

The spokesman shook his head. "Know nothing. What bad men do this?"

Joe did not answer the question. The Coast Guard officer thanked the Hardys and Sam Radley for their help, then the three departed. The operative decided to return to Windward. He would wait for the Federal authorities and give them all available information on the case.

The boys went to the Bayport Hotel and immediately got in touch with their father in Washington. He was delighted with the turn the case had taken, and promised to fly home at once. He would ask Mr. Delhi, who had arrived from New York the day before, to accompany him. Working together, the detective said, they ought to be able to locate Tava and wind up the case.

When the call was completed, Frank said, "Joe, I have a hunch we can find the mainland hideout by the time Dad and Mr. Delhi get here."

"How?"

Frank indicated the three cages with the pigeons in them. "We'll turn these birds loose from three different parts of the surrounding countryside and keep an eye on them with our glasses. If we map their lines of flight, they'll serve as bases for a triangulation fix."

"That's a swell idea," Joe agreed, "but first let's have lunch. I'm starved."

Immediately after a hearty meal, the boys began their work. Joe found a piece of paper, similar to those on which the other messages had been written, and printed:

SIT TIGHT. EVERYTHING OKAY THIS END.

He folded the message and inserted it in one of the capsules they had collected.

Meanwhile, Frank had hurried to see their jeweler friend. Mr. Bickford supplied him with four imitation rubies that would lull the suspicions of the kidnappers until the showdown.

When Frank returned, he and Joe went to the

roof of the hotel. From there they released the first pigeon with the message capsule. The boys watched the bird circle, then they lined up its course with a compass and marked the exact direction.

They divided the rubies between the two remaining pigeons. Joe took one bird five miles north of Bayport while Frank went five miles south with the other. When the boys returned to the hotel they compared notes and marked the chart again. Both grinned in satisfaction as they looked at the spot where the three lines crossed.

"I guess we've pinpointed the hideout," said Frank. "It's at the top of Lion Mountain."

The almost inaccessible spot was about twenty-five miles from Bayport, and it was reputed that mountain lions once had inhabited it. A few years ago the boys had climbed to the top and knew that it was a rugged hike.

"Frank," Joe said, "I think you and I should investigate Lion Mountain at once."

"You mean not wait for Dad?"

"We can't wait, Frank. If Bangalore and Nanab learn that Flont has been captured, and realize their whole plot is falling apart, I'm afraid they'll take revenge on Tava!"

"You mean kill him?"

"Yes."

Frank nodded. "We'll go at once."

CHAPTER XIX

Confessions

THE boys told their mother of the proposed plan and gave her the pinpointed map for Mr. Hardy. She said she would agree to their going only on one condition. They were to do nothing more than try to get word to Tava and help him to escape.

"Leave the capture of those smugglers and kidnappers to your father and the police," she said.

Frank and Joe promised they would. As they were about to depart, a telephone call came from Radley, who reported that the two men who ran the dory had been captured while docking it at Daly's lobster pound.

"Well, that settles everything at this end," the operative said. "I'll be back shortly."

The boys told him their plan, and he wished them luck. When they arrived at the near side of Lion Mountain, Frank parked the convertible where it would not be spotted and they started off on foot.

"I wonder how near the top the hideout is," Frank remarked. "Think we'd better circle the mountain to see if we can pick up a clue?"

"Yes. But I'll bet it's near the summit," said Joe.

"On the other hand," Frank said, "they might be nearer the bottom so that they could get away in a hurry if necessary."

The boys had nearly completed the circle before they found a clue. It was an indistinct trail and led upward.

Frank and Joe proceeded cautiously, constantly on the lookout for any traps. Half a mile up the trail, Frank spotted a suspicious-looking pile of leaves and twigs in the path. Picking up a long stick, he gently poked at the leaves and uncovered a bear trap.

"Wow!" Joe said softly as Frank threw a stone at it, springing the trap. "Did the smugglers or some trapper set that?"

Frank thought that probably the smugglers had. Farther on, they came across an uprooted tree cleverly braced into position, with its roots and a taut rope stretched across the trail, covered with earth and leaves. But it was ready to fall on anyone who might happen to trip over the rope.

About a half mile from the top in an open section, the boys came to a barbed-wire fence. It was about eight feet high and the upper strands were tilted outward, making it almost impossible to scale.

"Look!" whispered Joe from the shelter of the trees. "That fence is electrified!"

"It probably has a charge heavy enough to knock a fellow out," Frank remarked. "I'll bet it sets off an alarm, too."

"What a way to be stymied," said Joe.

Frank looked through the fence, his eyes probing the trees beyond. No one was in sight.

"What do you say we pole-vault over, Joe? Eight feet isn't too high."

"We'll do it," Joe said with determination. "About a hundred yards back I saw some saplings that had blown down. We can use them."

He located two stout saplings which suited their purpose. One he tossed over the fence to use when coming back. Meanwhile, Frank had dug a heel hole just short of the fence and braced it with flat stones.

"I'll go first," said Joe.

"Be careful," Frank warned. "Don't hit that fence!"

Joe ran forward lightly, hit the heel hole with a slight thud, and whipped up and over the fence. Frank grabbed the pole to keep it from striking the barrier.

Frank's jump was a bit trickier than Joe's, because he had to thrust back on the pole to keep it from hitting the fence and sounding the alarm.

The boys knew the hardest part of their job lay ahead. Through the scrubby bushes and trees they could see several crudely constructed huts. Near one of them stood a handsome, pensive-looking youth about eighteen years old. He was holding a hooded goshawk. From the color of his skin and his characteristic features the Hardys were sure he was an Indian.

The boy must be Tava!

Some distance from the youth were several dark-skinned men. They were no doubt some of the smuggled Indians.

In the shelter of the trees, the Hardys crawled toward Tava. When they were close enough to talk to him without revealing themselves to the others, Frank called in a whisper:

"Tava!"

As the young man turned and stared, Frank smiled and went on quickly, "We are Frank and Joe Hardy, American friends sent here by your cousin Bhagnav."

The youth moved slowly toward the boys and asked in a low voice, "Why does Bhagnav send you here?"

"To rescue you from your kidnappers."

"But I was not kidnapped," Tava explained. "Evil men are after me, and my friends are protecting me."

"That's not true," Frank insisted. "Your father

has already paid a fabulous ransom in rubies for your return, but these people continue to hold you and demand more payment."

Tava still did not seem to be convinced. Finally Frank said:

"Your cousin and your friend Rahmud Ghapur are very much worried. Mr. Bhagnav has engaged my father and brother and me to search for you. Mr. Ghapur told us of the time when he saved you in the cheetah hunt. He's afraid that you're in much greater danger now."

The boy's eyes widened in surprise. He whispered the name Ghapur several times. Then he replied:

"If Rahmud Ghapur and my cousin sent you, then I will go with you."

"Act as if you were just strolling around and follow us," Frank directed.

The Hardys crawled away. The Indian followed slowly, laughing and talking to the goshawk all the while. When the three were well out of sight of the buildings, and close to the fence, Joe said:

"I'm afraid you'll have to leave the goshawk here for now. When your abductors learn of your disappearance, they'll start a search. We may become separated. If this happens, take our car and meet us at the Bayport Hotel. My mother and aunt are staying there. Ask for Mrs. Hardy." He added detailed directions about the location of their hidden car and directions for reaching the hotel.

Tava regretfully fastened his goshawk's leash to a tree, picked up the pole, and gracefully vaulted the fence. He moved off quickly into the shadows of the trees beyond. Joe, pole in hand, was getting set to make his jump when Frank heard someone running.

"Jump, Joe!" Frank whispered tensely. The next second, a lariat slapped over his shoulders and he was pulled back.

As he hit the ground, Frank caught a glimpse of his brother halfway up in his leap. But suddenly Joe was snatched violently in mid-air. Frank, his heart sinking, knew Joe had been lassoed, too.

A half-dozen fiery-eyed men gripped both boys roughly and dragged them toward one of the buildings. They were thrust through the doorway into a well-furnished room, and confronted by two young Indians who resembled each other strongly. One, however, had a scar on his chin.

Bangalore and Nanab!

"The Hardy boys!" Nanab gloated. "A fine catch indeed."

"What were you trying to accomplish here?" Bangalore demanded.

Joe tried to act casual as he replied, "We came to get details of your smuggling and kidnapping plot. But I don't suppose we'll find that out now."

Nanab smiled and said, "Why not? We're proud of what we've done. We've fooled your authorities for a long time. Except for you two young snoops, everything has run smoothly. But since you are our prisoners, we can tell you the full story, then arrange a convenient accident for you."

Bangalore nodded agreement and Nanab began his revelation. "Captain Flont and his crew used the *Daisy K* to smuggle aliens into Bayport."

So Ragu had been lying all the time!

"Captain Flont," Bangalore went on, "is a clever man and will not betray us."

Despite the gravity of the situation, the Hardys could hardly keep from smiling. It was plain that the two ringleaders were not aware of any of the arrests that had been made. Frank's message sent by the pigeon must have arrived. Now, if the boys could only keep the men talking long enough, their father and the police would have time to get there.

"We started making plans two years ago when my brother Bangalore came to America," Nanab went on. "We spread word to dissatisfied citizens of our country that legal entry into the United States was impossible. However, by paying us a large fee they could be brought in surreptitiously and protected by us."

"How could you protect them?" Frank asked.

"We got them jobs and arranged for their social activities," Nanab explained.

"The kidnapping was my idea," Bangalore declared. "Both rackets were worked with Windward as the relay station. The property was bought cheap by our American friends John Cullen and Arthur Daly. They fed and housed the aliens who came in on a special American-Far East freighter, the *Red Delta*. It made an unscheduled stop outside a port in India to pick up the men, and another a few miles from Windward to discharge them onto a dory."

"And who is the Mr. L who was going to squeal?" Frank asked.

Bangalore and Nanab bristled at this. Then Nanab remarked, "Mr. Louis is a friend of Captain Flont's. He owns the dory."

"How did you get the ransom to this country?" Frank asked. "Not by the *Red Delta*, too?"

"Oh, no," Nanab answered. "The ransom rubies were picked up in India, flown by private plane to Europe, and brought to America on an ocean liner which passed in the vicinity of Windward. To avoid customs, small pouches containing the stones were thrown off into Louis's dory by a ship's officer who is one of our group.

"Unfortunately, Louis kept too many of the second shipment for himself. When we exposed him, he threatened to squeal. That is why we are holding him a prisoner here."

"You leased Mr. Smith's hunting lodge under the name of Sutter," Frank accused Bangalore.

Bangalore nodded. "I wanted to impress young Nayyar and make him comfortable. When you boys discovered the place, we left it, telling him that this was to avoid the evil men who were after him. He readily agreed to the move."

"You were staying at the lodge, too?" Joe asked.

"Oh, yes," Bangalore leered. "I was the one who knocked out your fat friend. One of the guards did the same to you," he said, looking at Frank. "When you found out too much, Nanab quit his job in Washington and came up here."

"And you, Nanab, destroyed the letter Mr. Ghapur sent us, but why did you let the falcon be shipped to us?" Frank queried.

Nanab smiled with self-satisfaction. "I was in charge of sending it. I could have destroyed the bird, too, but Ghapur would have realized I was responsible if you never received it. So I let it go through, then commissioned Ragu to steal it. He failed! He is a fool!"

"You also threw the bomb into our house and stole the falcon," said Joe. "But who set our boathouse on fire and jammed the *Sleuth*'s gas gauge?"

"I did," Bangalore admitted. "And now that you know the whole story, we will carry out our original plan."

He clapped his hands and several men stepped into the room. In their hands were sturdy rawhide whips!

"You're going to flog us first?" Frank shouted.

An evil smirk on his face, Bangalore said, "We usually plan a quick death with a sleeping potion for our enemies. But because you boys have caused us a great deal of trouble, Nanab and I have decided we will not make it so painless. Before you are put to sleep, we will use these whips and watch you squirm!"

"You're a bunch of sadists!" Joe cried out in protest.

"You won't get away with this!" Frank added.

Bangalore raised his hand, looked at the boys with a sinister smile, and said, "Flog them!"

CHAPTER XX

A Touch-and-Go Triumph

FRANK and Joe were seized by four guards, while two others raised their whips. But the boys did not flinch.

Instead, Frank leaned toward Joe. "Here we go again!" he whispered.

A knowing smile crossed Joe's face. Frank's statement was their secret signal for action. Before the whips could descend, the Hardys, using a jujitsu twist, flung their would-be floggers to the floor and tore the whips from the men's hands. The guards shrank back as the boys raised the whips.

Bangalore's jaw dropped. "How did you do that?" he asked, amazed, then added, "I like your courage. My men are skilled in wrestling, but you took them by surprise. It will entertain me to have you demonstrate your skill. Perhaps it can save you a flogging—or maybe even your lives."

Frank and Joe knew that Indians are great

lovers of the sport of wrestling. If they could prolong a match, their father might arrive in time to rescue them.

"We accept," Frank said. "But let's not decide our fate on a single fall. That's not sporting. We'll make it two out of three."

Bangalore laughed raucously. "You are prisoners, yet you make the terms!"

Nanab spoke up. "Let our men punish them in the manner they suggest," he said. "We'll teach them that Indians are the greatest wrestlers."

"Two out of three falls it is!" Bangalore conceded. "We will go outside," he said, leading the way.

As Frank and Joe laid aside the whips, the smugglers selected two lithe, smooth-muscled guards. In a crouched position they moved forward quickly, hands outstretched. But Frank and Joe were ready. Playing for time, they moved carefully, darting in, and then leaping back in an effort to catch their adversaries off balance.

Joe was first to find an opening. Seizing his opponent's left wrist, he spun him around, and pulling with all his strength, sent the man flying over his shoulder. The guard landed on his back, groaning as Joe leaped on him and applied a pinning hold that in a moment gave Joe his first fall.

Frank's foe cast his eyes on his defeated partner for a fraction of a second. With the speed of a stooping falcon, Frank charged, catching his adversary in a leg trip. The man hit the ground hard but jumped up quickly. Before he recovered, Frank caught him in a headlock that sent both sprawling in the dirt. There was a flurry of dust as the two fought savagely for the advantage.

Suddenly the guard's powerful legs closed about Frank's stomach in a crushing scissors grip. Frank tried in vain to break the tightening hold. As the guard pressed Frank's shoulders nearer and nearer the ground, it appeared that the boy would lose his first fall.

Then the guard shifted his hold slightly to make the pin. Frank, in spite of his weakened condition, saw his advantage and using all his strength he twisted free. Before his surprised opponent could recover, he spun around and seized the guard in a powerful cradle hold and drove him into the ground for a fall.

"Ready for the second fall?" Frank asked, breathing deeply.

The beaten man looked toward Bangalore and jabbered imploringly. The ringleader scowled and replied in their native tongue. Then, while the boys were resting, the Indian leader called forward two more guards.

The Hardys were to have new opponents for each fall! They realized it would be senseless to object.

When time was called, they approached their new rivals, and from the start it was apparent that the Hardys had the upper hand through their knowledge of the ancient Japanese art of jujitsu. In the midst of the second fall, a guard ran up, shouting:

"Tava! He is gone! I cannot find him anywhere!"

For a moment everyone froze. Then Bangalore screamed, "This is a trick! And you Hardys are responsible. You must die at once. Nanab, the potion!"

Guards swarmed around Frank and Joe, pinning the boys' arms back, so that they would be unable to resist. Nanab passed one of the poison pellets to his brother. He and Bangalore took up positions before the Hardys, forced their heads back, and pried open their jaws.

With all eyes on the scene, it came as a shock when a voice commanded, "Hands up!"

Fenton Hardy stood at the edge of the clearing. With him were Mr. Delhi, Ghapur, and Radley and several police officers. As everyone turned, a State Police captain announced:

"You're all under arrest!"

The ringleaders and their guards were quickly seized and handcuffed. Then the officers went to round up the smuggled Indians.

Mr. Hardy ran up to his sons. "Are you all right?"

"Yes," Frank assured him. "And we rescued Tava. He's on his way to the hotel."

"Wonderful!" cried Mr. Delhi and Ghapur.

A search of the premises was instituted at once. Under the floorboards in Bangalore's bedroom they found the cache of rubies.

"Amazing!" Ghapur commented.

"Enough evidence for a conviction on the kidnapping charge!" Mr. Hardy declared.

After the police left with the prisoners, the Hardys picked up Tava's goshawk and with their friends hurried to Bayport. When they reached the hotel, Tava was in the Hardy suite with Mrs. Hardy and Aunt Gertrude. Hugs, handshakes, and bowing followed with fervor and profusion. During the happy celebration Mr. Delhi and Rahmud Ghapur expressed their relief at finding Tava healthy and unharmed.

After the Indian youth had recounted his adventures, he motioned his countrymen aside and conversed in their native tongue. Rejoining the others, he explained that they were trying to decide on some fitting reward for the Hardys other than the usual fee for services, plus expenses which Mr. Hardy would be paid.

The entire family protested, but Tava turned to Mrs. Hardy and bowed. Then he took off his handsome ruby ring and presented it to her.

"Please accept this token of my deep gratitude," he said with a gentle smile. "I give it to the mother of the two bravest boys I have ever known."

Mrs. Hardy accepted the gift graciously. Later the whole group went to dinner in the hotel dining room. Even precise Aunt Gertrude enjoyed the victory celebration.

Early the next morning Chet Morton burst into his friends' room, demanding to hear the whole story. As they finished it, a cablegram was delivered to Frank and Joe.

"Listen to this," Frank cried excitedly. "It's from Satish Nayyar!" He read aloud:

" 'Cannot thank you enough for aid to my son. Tava is to continue his schooling. When he returns home next summer, will you accompany him and bring the boy who helped you?' "

"That's me!" cried Chet. "Wow, some reward!"

The three boys beamed. "We'll go!" Joe declared. "What a whale of an invitation!"

When the group gathered for breakfast, Frank and Joe told their parents about the cablegram. Mr. and Mrs. Hardy heartily approved of their sons accepting the invitation. Silently the boys wondered if the next mystery they would solve would be in India. But long before the following summer arrived, they became involved in *The Clue in the Embers*.

After the excitement died down, Mr. Bhagnav said, "I must explain something to Frank and Joe. I understand my leaving in such a hurry after the bombing gave you cause to wonder about my motives." He laughed. "My trip to New York was to meet another cousin of mine before he could be kidnapped!"

Frank and Joe smiled broadly. After a pause, Mr. Ghapur said:

"I have a gift of my own to offer—the falcon. I want you boys to keep the noble, courageous bird."

Frank and Joe accepted with alacrity, and added, "It would have been pretty hard to part with our hooded hawk."

Chet grinned. "Well," he said, "I guess the least I can do is treat you fellows to that dinner I promised. How about all of you coming out to the farm for a big celebration?"

Everyone accepted.

"And bring the falcon with you," Chet urged.

Joe grinned. "We will, if you'll have a pound of raw beef ready for Miss Peregrine as her reward."

Chet readily agreed. "But for all she did, the falcon deserves the best steak money can buy!"

"You're right," Frank said. "Without her, we couldn't have solved the mystery."

"Bravo, Miss Peregrine!" Joe said.

And Tava echoed, *"Shabash!* Bravo!"

Order Form
New revised editions of
THE BOBBSEY TWINS®

In *hardcover* at your local bookseller OR
simply mail in this handy order coupon and start your collection today!

Please send me the following Bobbsey Twins titles I've checked below.

AVOID DELAYS   Please Print Order Form Clearly

❑ 1	Of Lakeport	($5.95)	448-09071-6
❑ 2	Adventure in the Country	($5.95)	448-09072-4
❑ 6	On a Houseboat	($4.95)	448-09099-6
❑ 7	Mystery at Meadowbrook	($4.50)	448-09100-3
❑ 8	Big Adventure at Home	($4.50)	448-09134-8

Own the original exciting
BOBBSEY TWINS® ADVENTURE STORIES
still available:

❑13   Visit to the Great West   ($4.50)   448-08013-3

**VISIT PUTNAM BERKLEY ONLINE
ON THE INTERNET: http://www.putnam.com/berkley**

Payable in U.S. funds. No cash accepted. Postage & handling: $3.50 for one book. $1.00 for each additional. Maximum postage $8.50. Prices, postage and handling charges may change without notice. Visa, Amex, MasterCard call 1-800-788-6262, ext. 1, or fax 1-201-933-2316.

Or, check above books
and send this order form to:

**The Putnam Publishing Group
P.O. Box 12289, Dept. B
Newark, NJ 07101-5289**

Please allow 4-6 weeks for delivery.
Foreign and Canadian delivery 8-12 weeks

Book Total $ _____

Applicable Sales Tax $ _____
(CA, NJ, NY, GST Can.)

Postage & Handling $ _____

Total Amount Due $ _____

The Bobbsey Twins® series is a trademark
of Simon & Schuster, Inc. and is registered
in the United States Patent and Trademark Office.

Bill my: ❑ Visa ❑ MasterCard ❑ Amex _____(expires)

Card#_____
                                            ($10 minimum)
Daytime Phone # _____

Signature_____

Or enclosed is my: ❑ check   ❑ money order
SHIP TO:
Name _____
Address _____
City _____ State _____ Zip _____
BILL TO:
Name _____
Address _____
City _____ State _____ Zip _____

Order Form
Own the original 58 action-packed
HARDY BOYS MYSTERY STORIES®

In *hardcover* at your local bookseller OR
simply mail in this handy order coupon and start your collection today!

Please send me the following Hardy Boys titles I've checked below.
All Books Priced @ $5.95

AVOID DELAYS   Please Print Order Form Clearly

❏ 1 Tower Treasure	448-08901-7	❏ 30 Walling Siren Mystery	448-08930-0
❏ 2 House on the Cliff	448-08902-5	❏ 31 Secret of Wildcat Swamp	448-08931-9
❏ 3 Secret of the Old Mill	448-08903-3	❏ 32 Crisscross Shadow	448-08932-7
❏ 4 Missing Chums	448-08904-1	❏ 33 The Yellow Feather Mystery	448-08933-5
❏ 5 Hunting for Hidden Gold	448-08905-X	❏ 34 The Hooded Hawk Mystery	448-08934-3
❏ 6 Shore Road Mystery	448-08906-8	❏ 35 The Clue in the Embers	448-08935-1
❏ 7 Secret of the Caves	448-08907-6	❏ 36 The Secret of Pirates Hill	448-08936-X
❏ 8 Mystery of Cabin Island	448-08908-4	❏ 37 Ghost at Skeleton Rock	448-08937-8
❏ 9 Great Airport Mystery	448-08909-2	❏ 38 Mystery at Devil's Paw	448-08938-6
❏ 10 What Happened at Midnight	448-08910-6	❏ 39 Mystery of the Chinese Junk	448-08939-4
❏ 11 While the Clock Ticked	448-08911-4	❏ 40 Mystery of the Desert Giant	448-08940-8
❏ 12 Footprints Under the Window	448-08912-2	❏ 41 Clue of the Screeching Owl	448-08941-6
❏ 13 Mark on the Door	448-08913-0	❏ 42 Viking Symbol Mystery	448-08942-4
❏ 14 Hidden Harbor Mystery	448-08914-9	❏ 43 Mystery of the Aztec Warrior	448-08943-2
❏ 15 Sinister Sign Post	448-08915-7	❏ 44 The Haunted Fort	448-08944-0
❏ 16 A Figure in Hiding	448-08916-5	❏ 45 Mystery of the Spiral Bridge	448-08945-9
❏ 17 Secret Warning	448-08917-3	❏ 46 Secret Agent on Flight 101	448-08946-7
❏ 18 Twisted Claw	448-08918-1	❏ 47 Mystery of the Whale Tattoo	448-08947-5
❏ 19 Disappearing Floor	448-08919-X	❏ 48 The Arctic Patrol Mystery	448-08948-3
❏ 20 Mystery of the Flying Express	448-08920-3	❏ 49 The Bombay Boomerang	448-08949-1
❏ 21 The Clue of the Broken Blade	448-08921-1	❏ 50 Danger on Vampire Trail	448-08950-5
❏ 22 The Flickering Torch Mystery	448-08922-X	❏ 51 The Masked Monkey	448-08951-3
❏ 23 Melted Coins	448-08923-8	❏ 52 The Shattered Helmet	448-08952-1
❏ 24 Short-Wave Mystery	448-08924-6	❏ 53 The Clue of the Hissing Serpent	448-08953-X
❏ 25 Secret Panel	448-08925-4	❏ 54 The Mysterious Caravan	448-08954-8
❏ 26 The Phantom Freighter	448-08926-2	❏ 55 The Witchmaster's Key	448-08955-6
❏ 27 Secret of Skull Mountain	448-08927-0	❏ 56 The Jungle Pyramid	448-08956-4
❏ 28 The Sign of the Crooked Arrow	448-08928-9	❏ 57 The Firebird Rocket	448-08957-2
❏ 29 The Secret of the Lost Tunnel	448-08929-7	❏ 58 The Sting of the Scorpion	448-08958-0

Also Available The Hardy Boys Detective Handbook   448-01990-6

VISIT PUTNAM BERKLEY ONLINE
ON THE INTERNET: http://www.putnam.com/berkley

Payable in U.S. funds. No cash accepted. Postage & handling: $3.50 for one book. $1.00 for each additional. Maximum postage $8.50. Prices, postage and handling charges may change without notice. Visa, Amex, MasterCard call 1-800-788-6262, ext. 1, or fax 1-201-933-2316.

Or, check above books
and send this order form to:

**The Putnam Publishing Group
P.O. Box 12289, Dept. B
Newark, NJ 07101-5289**

Please allow 4-6 weeks for delivery.
Foreign and Canadian delivery 8-12 weeks

Book Total	$ _____
Applicable Sales Tax (CA, NJ, NY, GST Can.)	$ _____
Postage & Handling	$ _____
Total Amount Due	$ _____

Nancy Drew® and The Hardy Boys® are trademarks of Simon & Schuster, Inc. and are registered in the United States Patent and Trademark Office.

Bill my: ❏ Visa ❏ MasterCard ❏ Amex _____(expires)

Card#_____
($10 minimum)

Daytime Phone # _____

Signature_____

Or enclosed is my: ❏ check ❏ money order
SHIP TO:
Name _____
Address _____
City _____ State _____Zip _____
BILL TO:
Name _____
Address _____
City _____ State _____Zip _____

DETACH ALONG DOTTED LINE AND MAIL IN ENVELOPE WITH PAYMENT

Order Form
Own the original 56 thrilling
NANCY DREW MYSTERY STORIES®

In *hardcover* at your local bookseller OR
simply mail in this handy order coupon and start your collection today!

Please send me the following Nancy Drew titles I've checked below.
All Books Priced @ $5.95

AVOID DELAYS   Please Print Order Form Clearly

☐ 1 Secret of the Old Clock	448-09501-7	
☐ 2 Hidden Staircase	448-09502-5	
☐ 3 Bungalow Mystery	448-09503-3	
☐ 4 Mystery at Lilac Inn	448-09504-1	
☐ 5 Secret of Shadow Ranch	448-09505-X	
☐ 6 Secret of Red Gate Farm	448-09506-8	
☐ 7 Clue in the Diary	448-09507-6	
☐ 8 Nancy's Mysterious Letter	448-09508-4	
☐ 9 The Sign of the Twisted Candles	448-09509-2	
☐ 10 Password to Larkspur Lane	448-09510-6	
☐ 11 Clue of the Broken Locket	448-09511-4	
☐ 12 The Message in the Hollow Oak	448-09512-2	
☐ 13 Mystery of the Ivory Charm	448-09513-0	
☐ 14 The Whispering Statue	448-09514-9	
☐ 15 Haunted Bridge	448-09515-7	
☐ 16 Clue of the Tapping Heels	448-09516-5	
☐ 17 Mystery of the Brass-Bound Trunk	448-09517-3	
☐ 18 Mystery at Moss-Covered Mansion	448-09518-1	
☐ 19 Quest of the Missing Map	448-09519-X	
☐ 20 Clue in the Jewel Box	448-09520-3	
☐ 21 The Secret in the Old Attic	448-09521-1	
☐ 22 Clue in the Crumbling Wall	448-09522-X	
☐ 23 Mystery of the Tolling Bell	448-09523-8	
☐ 24 Clue in the Old Album	448-09524-6	
☐ 25 Ghost of Blackwood Hall	448-09525-4	
☐ 26 Clue of the Leaning Chimney	448-09526-2	
☐ 27 Secret of the Wooden Lady	448-09527-0	
☐ 28 The Clue of the Black Keys	448-09528-9	
☐ 29 Mystery at the Ski Jump	448-09529-7	
☐ 30 Clue of the Velvet Mask	448-09530-0
☐ 31 Ringmaster's Secret	448-09531-9
☐ 32 Scarlet Slipper Mystery	448-09532-7
☐ 33 Witch Tree Symbol	448-09533-5
☐ 34 Hidden Window Mystery	448-09534-3
☐ 35 Haunted Showboat	448-09535-1
☐ 36 Secret of the Golden Pavilion	448-09536-X
☐ 37 Clue in the Old Stagecoach	448-09537-8
☐ 38 Mystery of the Fire Dragon	448-09538-6
☐ 39 Clue of the Dancing Puppet	448-09539-4
☐ 40 Moonstone Castle Mystery	448-09540-8
☐ 41 Clue of the Whistling Bagpipes	448-09541-6
☐ 42 Phantom of Pine Hill	448-09542-4
☐ 43 Mystery of the 99 Steps	448-09543-2
☐ 44 Clue in the Crossword Cipher	448-09544-0
☐ 45 Spider Sapphire Mystery	448-09545-9
☐ 46 The Invisible Intruder	448-09546-7
☐ 47 The Mysterious Mannequin	448-09547-5
☐ 48 The Crooked Banister	448-09548-3
☐ 49 The Secret of Mirror Bay	448-09549-1
☐ 50 The Double Jinx Mystery	448-09550-5
☐ 51 Mystery of the Glowing Eye	448-09551-3
☐ 52 The Secret of the Forgotten City	448-09552-1
☐ 53 The Sky Phantom	448-09553-X
☐ 54 The Strange Message in the Parchment	448-09554-8
☐ 55 Mystery of Crocodile Island	448-09555-6
☐ 56 The Thirteenth Pearl	448-09556-4

**VISIT PUTNAM BERKLEY ONLINE
ON THE INTERNET: http://www.putnam.com/berkley**

Payable in U.S. funds. No cash accepted. Postage & handling: $3.50 for one book. $1.00 for each additional. Maximum postage $8.50. Prices, postage and handling charges may change without notice. Visa, Amex, MasterCard call 1-800-788-6262, ext. 1, or fax 1-201-933-2316.

Or, check above books
and send this order form to:

**The Putnam Publishing Group
P.O. Box 12289, Dept. B
Newark, NJ 07101-5289**

Please allow 4-6 weeks for delivery.
Foreign and Canadian delivery 8-12 weeks

Book Total $ _____

Applicable Sales Tax $ _____
(CA, NJ, NY, GST Can.)

Postage & Handling $ _____

Total Amount Due $ _____

Nancy Drew® and The Hardy Boys® are trademarks
of Simon & Schuster, Inc. and are registered
in the United States Patent and Trademark Office.

Bill my: ☐ Visa ☐ MasterCard ☐ Amex _____(expires)

Card#_____
($10 minimum)

Daytime Phone # _____

Signature_____

Or enclosed is my: ☐ check ☐ money order
SHIP TO:
Name _____
Address _____
City _____ State _____Zip _____

BILL TO:
Name _____
Address _____
City _____ State _____Zip _____